BACKWATER CHANNEL

A KURT HUNTER MYSTERY

STEVEN BECKER

THE WHITE MARLIN PRESS

Copyright © 2018 by Steven Becker
All rights reserved.
No part of this book may be reproduced in any form or by any electronic or mechanical means, including information storage and retrieval systems, without written permission from the author, except for the use of brief quotations in a book review.

***

Join my mailing list
and get a free copy of my starter library
FIRST BITE
http://eepurl.com/-obDj

1

THERE WAS about an hour of daylight left and the tide had just turned. Getting advice about fishing spots from the Internet can be sketchy, but the crystal clear flat looked about right. The website claimed that the incoming tide on a new moon was best and I was close. Conditions were good; not perfect. The light could have been more overhead, and the moon a few days closer to new. A whole lot of other things that I hadn't thought of yet could or should have been. I was here now, despite the tongue-lashing I had just taken, and slipped over the gunwale of the park service's twenty-two-foot center console intent on putting it all behind me.

Biscayne Bay bonefish are a trophy, often bigger and scarcer than their more tropical counterparts. Enticing one to bite and bringing it to the boat without a guide is difficult, but that was my task. I had cut a deal with the Miami-Dade Medical Examiner. I needed a favor; he wanted a Biscayne Bay bonefish, so I agreed to be his guide and our trip was scheduled for the coming week. I had never caught a bonefish, so I had to learn fast.

I scurried across the shallow flat, shuffling my feet to scare off any stingrays. With the rod in one hand and the #4 Bonefish Bunny in the other, I let the twelve-foot leader trail behind me. Stopping every few feet to watch for tailing fish, I waded to a shallow area in the shadow of one of the chimneys from the Turkey Point power plant.

I stood ankle deep in water, just south of where the outflow from the fossil fuel generators was discharged. With the sand flat right here the area was like a fish magnet. The plant had both nuclear and traditional generating facilities and was the object of countless environmental groups' outrage, but there were fish here. Maybe a trophy-size fish.

My gaze shifted back to the water where a tail caught my eye and I watched the water carefully trying to forget the meeting I had just left. Working my upper body back and forth to get into a casting rhythm, I stripped about sixty feet of line; ten more than I estimated I needed to reach my prey. Turning at an angle so as not to let the shadow of the line spook the fish, I started false casting. Swinging the line back and forth, without touching the water, I allowed the momentum from each cast to pull more line into the air. I had about forty feet out, when I double-hauled the rod and soon had the entire length in the air.

This was where it usually fell apart. Casting this much line was tough. I was lucky the wind was light, and turned back slightly to concentrate on the tailing fish. With one more back cast, I released the rod forward and held my breath while I watched the line extend in front of me. One of two things could happen now: the leader would either extend gracefully, dropping the fly silently on the water in front of the fish, or it would land in a pile of monofilament and spook him. Mine chose the latter and I watched the wake of the fish as it swam away. Defeated, I retrieved the line.

Returning to my starting position, I scanned the water looking for another fish. Beneath the lightly rippled water I saw another shadow, but realizing it was a cloud passing overhead, I continued scouting. Fishing with no expectations was fun for me. It was also how I approached my job. Yes, I caught my fair share of fish once I learned the waters, but that was only part of my reason for fishing. Having something to concentrate on opened my eyes to nature, allowing me to see things differently. Sometimes this was good and other times bad. It was how I had found two dead bodies in Biscayne Bay and a large pot grow in my previous posting at the Plumas National Forest in Northern California.

I hoped today would be different and I could toss a couple of flies and relax. So far, it was working. I could feel my breath and pulse slowing down and syncing with nature. This surprised me after my afternoon meeting with Martinez and the ever-present Susan McLeash. Martinez was the special agent in charge; Susan and I both held the title special agent, although she was clearly higher on Martinez's list than I was. I assumed it was her penchant for paperwork that soothed his bureaucratic soul. There were also rumors she satisfied some other parts of him, but I had no knowledge of this and held little regard for the coconut telegraph.

We'd just wrapped up the after-action report on my last case; a body I had found while fishing. Her name had been Abbey. Perhaps because I knew her name, it had become personal and I was glad that I was able to get her some justice. Unfortunately, both of the primary suspects ended up dead, one by Susan's rifle. That ended the official investigation even though it didn't solve the case. I prodded around a little on my own, but soon realized it was pointless.

Now the blame game had started. Susan claimed she had shot the woman to save my life; some of the eyewitnesses disagreed. Martinez kept a spreadsheet filled with numbers showing what the investigation had cost the park service. He also kept a "Kurt Hunter" file documenting every misstep I had taken since being assigned here. This was how he rolled. If it wasn't on a spreadsheet or included in his budget, it didn't matter.

I had no choice but to sit there and listen to him rant about me going off the reservation, drawing Susan into a dangerous situation, and upsetting the columns and rows on his spreadsheet. I bit my tongue, especially about Susan, hoping the whole time that I wouldn't miss the tide.

I'd barely made it and had come out at the slack and, now an hour later, I could feel the tug of the outgoing tide on my bare legs. This was a good sign. I just needed to find a willing fish before the sun set. In the deeper water, I heard some mullet jumping. Turning to look, I saw the telltale small circles emanating from the tail fin of a bonefish as it poked the sandy bottom looking for shrimp.

I never understood why the sun always looked bigger before it sank below the horizon, and now the huge orange orb seemed to balance on the mangroves in front of me. It would be dark in fifteen minutes and I suspected this would be my last chance at catching a fish today. Just a I thought it, a small wake appeared in front of me. I began to stalk the fish, carefully wading toward it and trying to get into range without spooking it.

The bonefish stopped near the roots of the mangrove-lined shoreline and resumed its search for food. This close to the shore, I had to be careful with my cast, but the trade off for the low hanging limbs was that the noise and activity in the branches and roots of the mangroves would cover my inexperience. Still fifty feet away, I stopped and allowed the fly to drop quietly onto the water while I stripped line off the reel. The small channel was sheltered from the wind and the water was a glassy calm. It would take a perfect cast to nab the fish. I started false casting and when the full length of line was in the air, I concentrated on keeping my wrist straight and released the fly. That one correction allowed the leader to unfurl naturally and the fly dropped about a foot from the nose of the fish.

Bonefish are notoriously sensitive and I froze when the fly made a small ripple that I thought might have been big enough to scare him. With the light fading fast, I started stripping line back. A few inches at a time I slowly retrieved the line, giving it a twitch with the rod tip every few seconds to give the fly some action, making it look like a real shrimp.

Suddenly, the fish turned. I thought I had lost it, but then the line went tight. This close to the mangroves, I had to get it on the reel quickly or it would escape. Working with both hands, I was able to hold the line tight and keep the fish out of the tangle of roots with my left hand while using my right to reel the excess line at my feet onto the reel. Getting that far without losing the fish was an accomplishment. Taking a deep breath, I released the line with my left hand and transferred the fight exclusively to the rod and reel. Leverage and drag beat hand lining any day.

Then the line went slack and in two heartbeats I knew the fight was over. I shook my head in disgust. Even though I had justified this as a scouting trip, it still hurt to lose one—especially a bonefish. Deflated, I started to reel in the line when I saw a pair of headlights coming toward me. The vehicle turned onto the embankment, which led behind a clump of mangroves adjacent to the cooling canals, where I heard it stop.

Figuring it was a maintenance vehicle, I ignored it and retrieved the line. I was about to head back to my boat when I heard a splash, some loud grunts and a scuffle. The noise stopped and two voices reached me, aided by the offshore breeze—a man and a woman—and although I couldn't tell what they were saying, they were clearly fighting. The woman yelled something to the man and I heard a door slam. Seconds later, the other door slammed and the engine started. I heard gravel spewing in the air as the vehicle screamed away.

2

I STOOD THERE WATCHING the sunset, knowing something had just happened—probably something I should be concerned about. I'd been stationed at Biscayne National Park going on four months now. The seasons had changed from the summer months, aka Hell, to the milder winter, which most people would describe as summer. During that time, I had learned a few things about the politics of the park service. Roy Martinez was my direct supervisor with the title: special agent in charge. I was merely a special agent.

Susan McLeash was my counterpart, though I don't think she had gotten that memo. An impartial observer would have thought she ran the whole show. Mariposa, the Jamaican receptionist and peacemaker, filled out the headquarter's staff. I lived in a park service house on Adams Key, one of the miles-long chain of islands that provided a natural barrier between the Atlantic Ocean and Biscayne Bay. The small island had two campgrounds and a day use area. Ray and his family were my only neighbors. Ray's job was to keep the outer islands running. He was the glue that kept everything working in the park; an ecosystem that fought off man— tooth and nail.

The area that was now Biscayne National Park had been slated for development in the fifties and sixties. There are still signs left of what had been started, but except for the few remaining buildings at Stiltsville, a community built in open water that was ravaged by Hurricane Andrew, there remain only some deep-water channels that end abruptly with nothing to show for the dredgers' efforts. The sea had taken the rest back.

I had no idea what I had just heard yet was sure it had happened on Florida Power and Light's property. That put it out of my jurisdiction, but things are not so simple here. The water connects everything and what comes in with the tide goes out with the tide. In all likelihood, if I just sat through the tide change, whatever I had heard thrown into the canal would eventually make its way into the bay.

The sun had slipped below the horizon and the short twilight of the sub-tropical latitude was well underway when I reached my boat and climbed aboard. Leaning against the seat, I checked my phone and had to admit I was disappointed to find no text or voicemail from Justine. My watch showed it was close to seven. She could be busy. Working the swing shift, from two to midnight at the Miami-Dade crime lab was hit or miss. Some nights, we talked or texted for hours, others she was so absorbed in work I never heard from her. It might have bothered me if I were a paranoid kind of guy, but I liked to think my own brand of craziness was also work-related.

I sent a quick, no pressure text to say hi, and put the phone in the waterproof glove box. I was curious about the recent disturbance and, with no other plans, raised the Power-pole that anchored the boat in shallow water, and started idling closer to the outflow. Darkness descended and I became more in tune with my surroundings. Noises that I wouldn't ordinarily notice during the day jumped out at me. Whenever sunset or sunrise coincides with moving water, things are usually pretty active. To make this official, a large school of baitfish broke the surface of the water beside the boat.

With no word from Justine and having no other plans, I dropped the Power-pole, anchoring the boat just short of the outflow, grabbed my rod, and started casting toward the mangroves, rationalizing my efforts as a patrol of the shoreline. If I had little expectation of catching that bonefish earlier, I really had none tossing a fly into the ink black water at night. Even though I was getting no bites, it was still fun.

From my position you couldn't help but notice the incongruence of Biscayne Bay. It is especially visible at night. Behind me, the power plant was lit up like a Christmas tree and looking up and down the coast I saw a small glow to the west from Homestead and further to the north the brighter lights of Miami trying to chase away the darkness. The pristine bay was hemmed in by man.

Nothing was happening so I flipped the switch for the underwater lights and looked over the gunwale. Fishing at night was a different game than during the day. Artificial lures and flies were generally ineffective. To lure a fish to the hook you needed another stimulus. Live bait, scent, or light worked. The blue LEDs lit the surrounding waters out to about ten feet and after a few minutes, I thought I saw the shadow of the predator that had scared up some smaller baitfish earlier, probably a barracuda. Then I saw something bigger.

The tide was still moving out, and I thought of that splash I had heard. I hadn't seen it, but guessed this was the area. Looking into the water I saw baitfish swarming around the object. It didn't take a trained special agent with my experience to identify it as a body.

An hour later, the water was lit by the reflection of the light bars from the Miami-Dade boats. One brought the coroner; the deputies on the other must have been having a slow night and run by to check out the floater.

"This fishing obsession of yours is trouble."

Sid's nasal whine cut through the night air. It was hard to tell with his New Jersey accent whether he was kidding or not, but we had been through two other bodies together and I knew that he had a wicked sense of humor.

"Just trying to get you some fresh air and exercise."

"Good for you," he said.

He was backlit by the searchlights, which were all focused on the body in the water that was now tied to the side of my boat. When I had found it I knew that I had to do something, or the two-knot-per-hour tide would carry it beyond the reef before morning, which may or may not have been the intention of the man and woman who had tossed it in. It had been a strange feeling, sitting there for an hour with a dead body tied next to me, but that was part of the job.

"Pass the line to the deputy and we'll take it from there," Sid called to me.

"Not so fast old man," I said. It was my body until someone told me otherwise. I knew this wasn't going to go well with Martinez, especially after he read my report that it was put into the water on FP&L land. He was a stickler for park service protocol and more than that, the preservation of his budget. I had brought him some good publicity on my prior cases, but he was still skeptical, and would place his chips on letting the body fall into another jurisdiction.

"Okay," Sid said. "You haven't lost your lunch yet, so consider yourself invited to sit in on the autopsy. Just bring your sweetheart."

We'd been through this before, and there was nothing that got Justine excited like a dead body. That should have given me cause for alarm, but since we had moved to a level three relationship, I was getting the feeling she liked the live ones too. "You're on. What time?"

"Let's call it midnight."

"I'll let Justine know."

While Sid and the deputy dropped fenders over the side and tied up to the park service boat, I snuck a quick text to Justine. It didn't take long for her response. The answer came back and I wondered where having to find her a dead body to get a date put her on the scale of high and low maintenance women.

"Swing the line around," the deputy called out.

I went to the transom, untied the line from the cleat, and walked it over to the Miami-Dade boat. Reaching up to hand it to him, I got a slight case of boat envy. The higher freeboard of the 27 Contender dwarfed the low gunwales of my twenty-two-foot bay boat. It wasn't really the size of the boat that excited me, but the array of electronics I saw at the helm. I knew my smaller center-console was the right choice for Biscayne Bay. My patrol area was mostly inside the barrier islands and protected. Shallow water was more of a danger than big waves, making the low draft bay boat a logical choice. Miami-Dade's coastline was primarily open water, making the larger Contender the better craft for them. Even so, those dual displays and radar would have been a nice addition to my ride.

Sid leaned over the side of the boat to check the body and called me over to help the deputy load it onto a backboard. It looked different than the last two I had found. This one had only been in the water a couple of hours, too soon for the crabs and fish to mangle it.

"Get the backboard," Sid said, taking the line from the deputy.

It looked like a two-man job and I crossed to the larger boat to help. Under Sid's supervision, which was mostly unnecessary, we had the body strapped to the board and hauled it over the side and onto the deck. A few small crabs climbed out of the crevices they had already found and scurried to the scuppers to make their escape.

"Good shape," Sid commented, taking the long probe and sticking it into the man's liver. He removed it and went to the console where the light was better to read the thermometer. He scratched his mostly bald scalp and looked like he was calculating something.

I took a quick look at the body now that it was out of the water. He was, or had been, a middle-aged man, now with a severely damaged leg. Sid cleared his throat and I pulled my notebook and pen from my pocket prepared to record whatever he said.

"I'm calling time of death between five and seven pm. It's a little vague with the body being in the water." He shined the flashlight on the man's bare leg. Crabs scurried from the deep ragged wound. "Odd's on that's the cause of death. Looks nasty."

The gash had torn through the femoral artery and exposed the bone; I expected he had bled out. A morbid thought came to me that if I had not found the body, the local denizens would have been attracted to the blood in the water. I was glad my fish box was empty.

I'd seen what eighty-degree water did to things. Time of death was an easier and more accurate calculation on land. Water buffered death's cooling effect and artificially kept the temperature higher for longer. I cursed myself for not noting the exact time when I heard the splash, but I was fishing.

Sid checked the man's pockets for ID, but came up empty. The liver probe was the only test that needed to be done on site and the deputy and I wrestled the corpse into a body bag. A few minutes later, I tossed the lines across and we separated.

My transportation needs had to be thought out ahead of time. In the past, I had made the mistake of relying on the boat, often docking at Dodge Island to get closer to Miami, and having to arrange for land transportation from there. Despite the traffic, taking the boat to headquarters and using my park service truck was a slower, but a better option.

I watched the Contender get up on plane and head slightly offshore to clear the shallow water around Key Biscayne before it would turn again for the entrance to Government Cut. After the wake had settled, I followed the shoreline to Bayfront Park and entered the channel. It was quiet this time of night, and I pulled into my slip at the park service dock, tied off the center console, and headed for the truck.

Dead body aside, I was glad I had an excuse to see Justine. As I started towards the truck, I wondered at the sanity of a relationship where you brought your girl a dead body instead of flowers.

3

I MET Justine at the doors of the Medical Examiner's office. I could see the excitement on her face, but when I leaned in for a quick kiss, I was denied. Her good mood was about the body, not me. Following her downstairs I got a glimpse of Sid through the glass partition. The body lay in its bag on the stainless steel table in the examining room where Sid hovered over it, going through his pre-game ritual. Justine went directly into the room. She leaned in and pecked Sid on the cheek. I didn't have those kind of privileges. Tapping the glass, I waited for him to acknowledge me before entering.

"Go ahead and suit up. You know the drill," he said, not looking up.

This was my third time around, and I wasn't sure if I should be happy or worried about how comfortable I was getting with death. I suspected it was easier in a laboratory environment. The stainless steel furniture and tile decor gave the room a clean clinical atmosphere. Though the smell of death still got to me.

Sid unzipped the body bag and revealed the dead man's face. The fresh stubble still glistened with bay water. His face looked human; the last two bodies I had found had been under long enough for the seawater and foragers to steal their identity, making the faces unrecognizable. The eyes of the recently deceased corpse made me fear for my stomach.

I waited, watching through my acrylic facemask, which fogged up slightly with each breath. From my previous experience, I knew I had some time. The first step was to do a visual inspection of the body. Sid nodded to Justine who turned on the voice recorder. When the red light went on, he began work.

"Male, age late thirties to early forties—"

The shrill ring of my phone echoed off the tile walls. Sid and Justine looked at me as if I had interrupted a sacred ritual and I stepped away from the table. It was the Darth Vader ring tone I had assigned to Martinez. I glanced down at the screen on my way out the door and noticed the time was twelve-thirty. There was no way this was anything but trouble.

"You're like a shit magnet, Hunter," he started.

I stepped out into the office to avoid interrupting Sid.

"Do these bodies just find you or do you seek them out?"

The line went quiet. It was time for me to respond. "I'm at the autopsy now." I figured he already knew where I was from the park service equipment. GPS trackers in the boat and car as well as software in my phone gave him a steady stream of information. This was his primary form of entertainment after golf. Why watch TV, when you can creep on your agents in real time? His office was equipped with dual large screen monitors that I had seen displaying the tracks of other agents. I could only imagine what his home setup looked like.

"You're what? Again, you're overstepping. The body came out of the cooling canals. That puts it on FP&L land and in Miami-Dade's jurisdiction. You're not on my clock."

His information confirmed my guess that it was Miami-Dade feeding him the information. I was used to working on my own time, which didn't bother me because it usually meant Justine was involved. A glance through the window to the autopsy room told me that Sid was not waiting for me. I looked back at the phone knowing that sooner rather than later there would be a face-off with my boss. I figured now was not a good time—the dark of night seldom was. Before I could answer that the body was actually found in the park, my phone beeped. "Hold on." He started to say something, but ignoring him, I looked down at the screen and saw "blocked caller ID".

"I'll check in first thing tomorrow," I said, switching calls before he could make the inevitable comment. "Kurt Hunter," I answered the other call.

"Agent Hunter, this is Grace Herrera with Miami-Dade. I'm the detective the case was assigned to." She waived the pleasantries. "Can you meet me and my partner at the Turkey Point plant? We want your take on what you saw."

I wondered how they knew what had happened already and remembered the deputy's in the other boat. I told Herrera that I was at the ME's office right now and would get down to Turkey Point as soon as I could. Through the glass partition I saw Sid about to make the Y-shaped incision and was almost thankful for the excuse to miss the rest of the autopsy. Still, I couldn't turn away when he winked at Justine, and with a flourish like a conductor signaling the first bars of a symphony, made the first cut. I turned away. Having your girlfriend see you lose your lunch is never a good thing.

"I'll have a security guard meet you at the gate. He'll bring you to the site." Herrera hung up.

I turned to go back to the door of the exam room when I saw Justine put her phone in her pocket and head toward me.

"Gotta go to the site," she said, tearing off the robe.

"Me too. Miami-Dade asked me to show them what I witnessed."

"I need to take the crime scene van. You have your truck. I'll meet you there."

I wondered if I should ask her to breakfast out at my place across the bay and decided against it. We were already walking a tightrope of what was professionally appropriate. I didn't want to add to it. Right now, I was a witness, and she had her job to do.

"Okay. I'll meet you there."

She glanced back at the exam room, leaned in and gave me a quick peck on the cheek. "This is so exciting!"

I let that go, knowing that it wasn't me that she was so jazzed about and headed up the stairs and out the front doors. The air was thick, a surprisingly humid night for this time of year. I had been through the summer and fall now, both of which would have been classified as summer anywhere else. Now it was early winter and we had seen our first few cold fronts. It was pretty nice this time of the year, although, once every ten days or so, the humidity returned which usually meant a front was coming. They often came through quickly and violently, bringing squall-like conditions. Once the line of storms passed the weather turned to what could only be described as outstanding, at least until the next one pushed through as the cycle of South Florida weather continued.

With that in mind, I looked up at the sky while I got in my truck. The first line of stratus clouds illuminated by the moon told me a storm was coming. I started out of the parking lot and headed toward the 836. I wasn't surprised when I saw the flash of brake lights on the on ramp. Miami is one of the true metropolitan cities in the US and there was still quite a bit of traffic even at this hour. Fortunately, the delay was due to some construction and short-lived. While I waited, I entered the plant's location into my phone. Following Siri's directions, forty minutes later, I reached the entrance to the Turkey Point power plant.

The Miami-Dade forensic van was already there, idling by the side of the road. I looked around, surprised to see there was no gate or guard for a nuclear facility. A pair of headlights appeared to be coming toward us. I pulled next to Justine's van and waited. As the vehicle approached, I could see right away that its headlights were too narrow for a standard car or truck. A uniformed security guard driving an off-road utility vehicle passed us and swung a quick U-turn. He waved to us and we followed him into the compound.

From the Palm Drive entrance we went through a parking lot, past a well-lit industrial building and turned right onto SW 360th street. On the right, invisible in the darkness, were the cooling canals.

Running perpendicular to the road, the ten-square-mile grid was laid out with hundred-foot-wide canals separated by earthen berms that looked to be about fifty feet in width. An outer canal running around the perimeter enclosed the entire system. We turned onto a crushed coral road. The UTV the security officer was driving handled the uneven surface better than my small two-wheel drive pickup and after five bone-jarring minutes, we made a sharp right turn and I found myself looking at the spot where I had started fishing earlier.

Another hard quarter mile later, we stopped near a canal close to the area where I thought I had heard the vehicle earlier. There was already a Miami-Dade cruiser pulled over to the side of the road. Its headlights illuminated two officers looking down at the gravel, scanning its surface with high-power flashlights. Justine drove the crime scene van towards them and stopped so that her headlights added to the cruiser's light. I parked well behind them and walked the rest of the way.

A gust of wind caught me by surprise and I looked up at the moonlit sky. To the north the line of ominous looking clouds I had seen earlier was getting closer; the front was coming at us fast. I approached the two officers, leaving Justine to do her own thing.

"Officer Herrera?" I asked.

One of the pair looked up and I saw a very attractive woman. Another gust blew, and I wondered if the gods were causing trouble when Justine looked up and saw me staring at the Miami-Dade detective.

"Call me Grace," she said.

Justine was still staring at us. I don't know why I felt so self-conscious, I had no reason to expect any kind of reaction from her. This was strictly business, though I realized I was still looking at Grace. Her partner continued to scan the ground illuminated by the headlights, not really caring about my demise. "Kurt," I said, moving toward her and shaking her hand.

"I'll need a statement," she said.

The wind kicked up again and we both looked at the sky. The line of clouds was even closer now, and in the flash of the first lightning strike I could see her face clearly. It only reaffirmed my previous opinion. In response, the slow, low rumble of thunder sounded like the throaty roar of an animal about to attack. "Maybe we better process the site first. This storm's gonna be here pretty quick." As if to confirm this, another gust hit us, this time stronger and colder.

"Looks nasty. Maybe you're right. While we're here though, I need you to show me where you were and where you heard the vehicle."

Grace waved to Justine who walked toward us carrying a bright flashlight and a camera. When she reached us I started toward the other officer.

"Looks like a UTV from the tires," he said. "Tracks are a little narrow for anything else."

"That's about the spot. I guess it could have been a UTV. I only heard the vehicle so I'm not sure." I started looking on my own for the tracks.

"Pretty sure, probably—huh?" he mimicked me. "I bet if it was a fish you park service boys could give a positive ID."

I was about to introduce myself, but pulled back. As if she knew her partner all too well, Grace intervened.

"Where were you fishing?"

I pointed out the spot where I had anchored and explained how I had waded by the mangrove-studded shoreline.

"Catch anything?" her partner asked.

I let that one go. This guy was trouble and I knew better than to engage him. "Miami mean" was what I called it. One of the first things I had noticed after moving here was that the east-coast attitudes were more sarcastic and harder to read. The wind blew again, laced with the first raindrops of the coming storm. Justine looked at me and we both turned toward the northern sky.

"This is all going to have to wait. We're going to lose this scene in about ten minutes." She started taking pictures of the general location and the tire tracks. "Can you guys fan out and see if there is any physical evidence we might lose because of the storm?"

I was grateful for the reprieve and pulled the Maglite from my belt. It was a smaller version of the foot-long lights the two police officers carried but still plenty bright. I walked toward the outside edge of the bank adjacent to the bay. Looking back at the group, I noticed a few scrubby trees. Thinking back, l thought the vehicle I had heard would have been near them and close to where I stood. Panning the banks, I saw the water was a few feet below the high-tide line. This was about the tidal range and I guessed any evidence would likely be beyond the reef by now.

I turned my attention to the crushed gravel road. Sweeping the light back and forth I saw some similar tire tracks, then I thought I saw something and moved toward it. The first fat drop of rain hit the back of my neck as I leaned over to inspect the area; something had happened here. I was about to take a picture with my phone when I saw a light approach.

"I'm going to need that statement," Herrera said. "Why don't you come down to the station."

I wasn't sure if that was a request or a command. We were only a mile or so from Bayfront Park and my boat. It had been a long day and I was getting anxious about the storm. Crossing the five miles of bay water to my home on Adams Key was generally an easy run in the protected bay waters. I had been out in twenty-plus mile per hour winds, it was already blowing close to that, and I feared there was worse to come.

"Can we go to the park service headquarters building?"

"Yeah. I think we're about wrapped up here. We can follow you."

Her partner said something, which I'm sure was aimed at demeaning me, but his words were lost in the thunder. The drizzle turned to rain and we all looked at each other knowing what was coming: it wouldn't be long before this would evolve into a full-fledged squall. I made it back to my truck before the sky opened and sat wondering, as I watched the rain pound against the windshield, where I was going to sleep tonight. I could wait out the storm at the headquarters building, but there was no telling how long the squalls were going to last. As if reading my mind, my phone vibrated in my hand. I pulled it out to find Justine's name on the screen. Realizing I hadn't said anything to her before we ran to our vehicles, I looked around and saw her sitting in her van just twenty feet from me. She made a face and I thanked the heavens for distracting her from Grace Herrera.

"Why don't you come up."

There was no deliberation. "I have to give Miami-Dade a statement first," I said and graciously accepted her invitation. There would be a warm bed to sleep in tonight. I looked at my watch. She would be off in an hour. I pulled onto the gravel embankment and waited until I saw headlights behind me before retracing the road. Then I remembered the tire tracks and the picture I had failed to take. Just as I was about to turn around, the rain increased. In seconds, the downpour had filled the potholes; any evidence would be gone by now.

Rationalizing that it wasn't my case anyway, I started driving along the rough road. Straining to see through the downpour and fogged windshield, I hit several water-filled potholes making for a much bumpier ride going back. The Miami-Dade cruiser's headlights bounced around wildly in my rearview mirror giving me at least some satisfaction that Grace's partner was taking the same beating.

Under normal conditions with the dead-straight roads and no traffic, the drive would take about ten minutes; less if you pushed it. In this weather, it took closer to twenty. We reached the turnoff, parked in the lot, and made a run for the headquarters building, reaching it just as the brunt of the storm hit.

Martinez had seen fit to issue me a key, saying I had survived my probationary period. I wasn't sure if there was some actual trust building between us, or if we had only reached a wary peace. My hands were slick with rain and I fumbled with the key as I tried to unlock the commercial style glass doors. Trying to ignore the grunts from Grace's partner, I finally succeeded and we went inside. I also had a key to my own vehicle and I pocketed the three keys; my house, truck, and office wondering what the size of a person's key ring said about their life.

The three of us stood in the lobby shaking off the rain as I searched the walls for a light switch. "How about we just sit here," I said, motioning to the couch and chairs set up as a waiting area in the lobby.

"Sure," Grace said, sitting on the couch.

The other detective took the chair. "Got any coffee?"

"Fresh out," I said, not about to embarrass myself further by trying to find and make some. "What can I help you with?"

Grace asked the questions and took notes while the other officer interjected snipes and comments whenever he could get a jab in. I wasn't sure how I ended up in a pissing match with him, but looking over at Grace, I had a feeling she had something to do with it.

Just as I finished answering their questions, a loud clap of thunder ended our meeting. I offered Grace one of the park service umbrellas sitting by the door. The detective shot me a nasty look, took his own, and they ran for their sedan just as the skies opened again. There was no point in going out now. Besides getting soaked myself, the visibility would be zero and the roads impossible until the storm abated. With nothing else to do but wait, I walked up the dark stairs to my office and saw the glow of Martinez's dual monitors from under his door. It was tempting to go in and see what he was connected to now, but I passed. He probably had a camera above his door to see who entered.

My office was an inside room in the corner. Thankfully there was a light switch that worked and in a place you would expect it. My computer also cooperated and booted up. In a few minutes I was logged into the Miami-Dade medical examiner's site. It turned out that my John Doe had a name.

4

THE STARK FLUORESCENT lighting in my office flickered and the building shook as I typed the dead man's name into the computer and waited, wondering how they had identified him so quickly. When the search page populated, I had my answer: Edward Ingerman, attorney from Miami, occupied the entire first and half the second page of the results. He had quite the resume as an environmental activist who leaned toward the radical side. There were at least a dozen articles about his exploits and subsequent arrests. With his record, there was probably a good chance that one of the detectives recognized him. I did a little creeping on his social media accounts but didn't turn up much more than the original search. If he had a family, he was carefully keeping them out of the public eye.

An environmental activist found dead in Biscayne National Park was not the headline that Martinez wanted to see when he woke up tomorrow. He would do everything in his power to push the case into Miami-Dade's jurisdiction, keep the park service out of it, and protect his budget from the disaster this could easily become.

A quick trip downstairs told me that the rain had stopped. The winter cold fronts, especially the strong ones were like this. A brief period of intense storms followed by a drop in temperature and humidity. From looking at the flags out front, I could tell the wind was still blowing close to twenty mph. If I had to, I could have made the wet run out to Adams Key, but I had a better offer. I locked up the office and headed to the truck. It was time to pay Justine a visit.

"Did you see the ID on the body?" she asked when I walked into her office a half hour later.

"Yeah, this is going to be high profile."

"How's your bossman going to react to an environmental activist being found dead in the park?"

"Just asking myself the same question." I gave her a peck on the cheek, our standard in-work greeting. "How much longer do you have to work?"

"I was hoping to finish with the forensics from Turkey Point."

And here was the line I had to try and maintain. At least she had brought it up, but I wasn't going to say no. I'd had trouble before keeping work and play separate, and was making a conscious effort not to wreck this relationship. "Your call," I said.

"We can leave if you want. The case will get assigned to the homicide division tomorrow. They won't be expecting anything until the day after."

I couldn't help myself. "I thought finding the body inside the park boundaries would give me a shot at it."

She gave me a knowing look, but then smiled. "Looks like our special agent from the NPS is a little bored with patrol duty."

I returned her smile, trying not to disclose how right she was. The park was beautiful, and I had gained a great amount of boating knowledge as well as become a passable fly fisherman in the past few months. But it was much like patrolling the national forest out west— mostly boredom and little action. Besides helping boaters stuck on the flats, the park was quiet. The remoteness of the campgrounds kept the rowdies out. When the closest liquor store was a five-mile boat ride plus a twenty-minute car ride away, the partiers often chose more convenient locations.

"The storm probably destroyed most of the evidence. We only

have tire prints and some random objects picked up at the site. It can wait."

Despite my initial reaction, the more I thought about it, the better I felt about letting this one go to Miami-Dade. With so little evidence and my statement that the body had been dumped in FP&L's cooling canals, there was little I could do. For once Martinez and I might be on the same side, and it wasn't going to hurt relations with Justine if I passed on this one.

———

THE ANGRY DARTH VADER RINGTONE WOKE ME THE NEXT MORNING, confirming my decision to let Miami-Dade have the body. I rolled over to ignore the call, and found the other side of the bed empty. The sun was up, Justine was gone, and Martinez was calling. I answered before the call went to voicemail, which would have only aggravated him further.

"You are a shit magnet," he started.

I passed on the response on the tip of my tongue and let him continue.

"I got an interesting call from FP&L this morning. It seems the director of the plant wants to meet the park service agent that found the body. Why is that?"

It didn't take me long to come up with an excuse because I didn't need to. "I have no idea. I gave my statement to the Miami-Dade officers on site and haven't done anything since." For once, I was able to tell him the truth.

"Well, whatever their reasons, you better get down here."

Of course, he knew where I was from the GPS tracker in the truck. "On my way," I said and disconnected. I got up and went to the kitchen where I found a cup of coffee left in the pot and a note from Justine that she had gone out for a paddle. Taking the coffee with me to the bathroom, I showered, dressed, and finished my morning caffeine dose. Fifteen minutes from when he called, I was on the road.

Going against rush hour traffic, I made good time to the park service headquarters. I must have been smiling when I walked in the door because Mariposa called me over to the reception desk.

"Kurt, you been seeing that new girlfriend?"

Justine and I had been dating for four months and Mariposa had invited me several times to come have dinner with her and bring the "new girlfriend." She had even sweetened the invitation by offering to break out her husband's best rum, but I had begged off every time and was starting to feel guilty.

"You know that offer to have dinner at your place? If it's still open for Saturday night, I'll ask Justine if she can make it."

"Yes suh, Mr. Kurt, that'd be about fine," she said sarcastically.

I wasn't sure if you could laugh with an accent, but she seemed to impart some of that Jamaican lilt into hers. "Good. No excuses and see you at seven. Better wipe that smile off your face and go see the boss. He's called down three times already to see if you're here yet."

I nodded to her. The smile was gone with the mention of his name, and I headed up the stairs. The door to Susan McLeash's office was closed and I almost smiled again at the thought of having missed that confrontation only to see her sitting across from Martinez in his office when I arrived. Actually, it was her perfect hair that I saw first. The forty-odd-year-old was a little too pressed and starched for my taste. Once probably a good-looking woman, her vanity had interfered with the aging process and now she looked contrived. Her wrinkle free uniform was a little too tight in the wrong places, her makeup coated her face into a mask that only allowed a scorn, and her hair was a solid block from too much product.

Martinez waved me in, forgoing any pleasantries.

I nodded at him and Susan, sat and waited for him to start.

"Florida Power and Light's counsel called a few minutes ago. They are adamant that the case stays in the park service's jurisdiction."

I was a little surprised. The body had been found in the park and they probably wanted to push any bad press away from them.

"I'm not going to tell you I'm happy about this, but I gather you've got a head start.'

"We have an identity." I pulled my notepad out to check the name. "Edward Ingerman. I did a quick search and found out he's an environmental activist."

"That doesn't play well. FP&L is wrapped up in all kinds of litigation about their operations affecting the water quality of the bay. The last thing they need is this kind of publicity."

"And they think we do?" I said, trying to be sympathetic. I caught a look of surprise from him. "Out west," I added, "we had our share of activists in the national forest."

"Right. So we have to watch our step here. I'm assigning Susan to work with you on this. It's going to take both of you to handle the media and solve the case."

Susan smiled. Martinez and I had gotten both credit and commendations for the last two cases. She had gotten none—only probation for the shooting. As I looked at her, I could only think of the old proverb about keeping your friends close and your enemies closer. Susan fell into the latter category. It would be better to be officially partnered with her than having her run freelance and disrupt the investigation.

Martinez looked up to dismiss us. We both looked at each other, but neither asked the question on both our lips: "Who was in charge?" Dismissed, we got up and I followed her out of Martinez's office.

"The counsel from FP&L wants to meet with us," Susan said.

If there was any doubt, that answered the question. Without Martinez saying my name out loud it would fall to her. She was senior to me and was the perfect agent, at least as far as her paperwork went. And, to a career bureaucrat like Martinez, looking at two or three years to retirement, it wasn't justice that was important but his clean exit and pension.

I walked out of the meeting determined to turn the tables.

5

On the way over to the Turkey Point plant Susan asked me to bring her up to speed, which I did, leaving out the reason I was by the plant in the first place. I was pretty sure she and Martinez knew that I fished, but it was not going to be me to confirm it.

"You know anything about this group Edward was affiliated with?" I asked.

She looked down at her notepad. "MACE, stands for Miami Alliance for Clean Energy."

I guessed that Martinez had given her a heads up on his intentions and she had been doing her homework before our meeting. I had some catching up to do. "What's their MO?"

"Lawsuits mostly," she started. "There's nothing I see that ties them directly to any violence, though they organize regular protests. It seems they focus almost solely on the Turkey Point plant."

"I guess someone's not so happy. It's quite a statement to toss one of their lead attorneys into the cooling canals."

"There are some other groups. I'll check that angle out."

So far, so good, was all I could think when we pulled up to the seventies-style office building. If she handled the research and paperwork, this might actually work, but it was an informal division of responsibility and I doubted she would stay inside the lines.

The greeting committee met us at the door. Two men and a woman stood inside the air-conditioned lobby. The cold front had moved south, taking the humidity with it and leaving a cloudless sky. Days like this are few and far between here, and I found it interesting that they waited inside. Then I saw the haircuts and suits. These were clearly attorneys sent to make sure we understood that this investigation was about an activist, not FP&L.

We introduced ourselves and after shaking hands and passing cards, they took us to a conference room. A huge table dominated the room and a large flat screen TV hung on the wall. Once we were seated and offered drinks, the lights dimmed and the screen lit up.

"We thought that a general overview of the plant and operations would help with your investigation," the woman said. Dressed more for a cocktail party than a presentation, she stood apart from her more conservatively dressed counterparts. She pointed a remote at a projector mounted to the ceiling and a video started playing.

It was clear that this was FP&L's version of how the plant was safe, environmentally secure, and a general benefit to the Miami area. It started with a short piece on the wildlife of the bay, showing herons, and fish. Then a piece on the American crocodile, which was narrated by a researcher in safari wear with a lot of letters following his name. Video of scientists tagging baby crocodiles almost convinced me the power giant cared.

Next the video moved onto images of South Florida taken from space at night. The first showed the lights along the coastline and the second mostly darkness taken after the eye of Hurricane Andrew passed over the plant in 1992. The narrator was sure to point out that the plant had only been closed for safety inspections and had not been damaged by the hundred and fifty plus mile an hour winds in the eye wall. Then the image of the glowing corridor from Palm Beach to Homestead replaced the black-out image to reinforce their point.

"So, you can see the impact of the plant on the area," she said after the video ended. "It is vital to our entire community for us to stay online."

I could see through the propaganda enough to know where they were going with this. Raising my suspicions with these folks would be counterproductive. What I really wanted was to get out of the office and take a dime tour of the place. "You said we could have a look around?"

"Of course, we will cooperate anyway we can," the woman said. "Rebecca Moore," she introduced herself and extended her hand, holding mine for just a second too long.

Her piercing blue eyes never left mine. Finally, she smiled and released me from her spell. We left the conference room and were met by a security guard.

"Bob here will show you around, please feel free to call me with any concerns or questions," Rebecca said, pausing to write her cell phone number on her card. She handed it to me. "Call me anytime."

She gave me a sultry smile, and the suits went back into the conference room to discuss how best to handle us.

"They're bringing out the big guns," Susan said.

"That guy was working you pretty hard too." I had seen her thumb the business card one of the men had handed her when we said goodbye. She smiled and put the card in her pocket. I wasn't the only one with a hand-written phone number.

"Where do y'all want to start?" Bob asked.

He seemed to be a likable enough guy without an agenda. The tension eased and we asked him for the full tour. I wanted to get a feel for how this place operated; what areas were secure and restricted. It seemed unlikely that anyone could just drive up to one of the cooling canals and dump a body.

I would like to say that the tour of the sprawling industrial complex that powered South Florida was fascinating, but it wasn't. Bob recited stats and figures that were probably contrived to impress, but they meant nothing to me. He guided us through the plant, greeting most of the workers and other guards by their first names. Out of courtesy I dutifully wrote down most of what he said. This guy knew everyone and everything that happened here. He could be useful.

There were a few takeaways that I also wrote down—several of which surprised me. You could drive up to most of the buildings. There were no gates or checkpoints, though entering some facilities required a badge. There were also very few people. I assumed there were cameras installed, but if you knew where they were, it might be possible to move around the facility without being seen.

"Can we have a look at the security videos?" I asked, pointing to a camera mounted under the eave of the building we just left.

"I reckon. There's not much on the canal system though."

We hopped into his UTV and headed to another building. "What's your take on all the protests and that MACE group?" I asked, trying to get a feel for how protective the employees were of the plant.

"You can't make those folks happy. We got the largest population of American crocodiles in the U.S. in those canals. Scientists, tagging programs—we got it all. Hell, there's hundreds of acres of FP&L property dedicated to the wildlife here. From what I understand, those crocs would be damned near extinct without us. Now they want to shut down the canals and use cooling towers. One thing I know is you can't butter your bread on both sides without it getting messy."

With the rant over, we pulled up to a small building. Bob opened the door with his security badge and we followed him inside. Seated at a long counter, were a man and a woman, both wearing the same uniform as Bob. A dozen monitors were mounted on the wall in front of them. Every ten seconds the camera angle changed.

"Y'all can see here we have coverage of all the sensitive areas," Bob said, pointing to the labels affixed to the bottom of each screen.

"Why not the canals?"

"Didn't think there was much of a reason, but they don't ask my advice. Maybe Ms. Moore can help you," he said, giving me a slight smile.

I think he almost winked when he said it. Ignoring the insinuation, I continued. "Do you patrol around there?"

He nodded, "Typically there's three of us on duty at a time. One is on the grounds and the other two keep an eye on things here. Miami-Dade is pretty responsive if there's anything we can't handle. It's a big place though."

"So, there's a good chance whoever was on the grounds last night when the body was dumped didn't see anything?" Susan asked.

I didn't like her tone. The way she asked the question was almost like telling them they weren't doing their jobs. "I saw headlights out on the far end of the system and it was pretty dark," I said, trying to smooth things over with him.

"There're miles of those canals, but it's all exposed ground. You can see damned near across it. Once in a while we'll see a tourist looking for a picture of a crocodile, and we used to get fisherman, but we've run them all off."

"Do you have a camera on any of the entrances?"

He cleared his throat. "Them lawyers you met before are pretty tight about releasing anything. Unless you have a warrant, I gotta talk to Ms. Moore and get permission."

"Shouldn't be a problem to get a warrant," Susan said, taking her phone out.

Again, she set the guards on edge. I glared at her and she put the phone back in her pocket. "Ms. Moore gave me her card. I can give her a call," I offered.

"Reckon that's the best way," Bob said.

I gave Susan another look telling her to keep quiet. "How about we take a run around the canals and we'll get out of your hair."

"Right behind you," Bob said, motioning us toward the door.

The front door was locked and I paced, waiting for Bob. I wanted to scold Susan, but thought it better to wait until we were out of earshot. The floor in front of the door was tiled and I felt something in my boot. Sitting on a bench, I crossed my legs and pulled a piece of gravel that was stuck between the lugs. Bob joined us a long minute later, unlocked the door, and led us back to the off-road vehicle.

"Thirty-six canals in all. Water takes two days to cool down," Bob said as he pulled out.

He repeated many of the same facts we had already heard. Susan and I were white knuckled from grabbing the roll bar as Bob navigated around the water-filled potholes. When I wasn't grabbing the safety rail I looked around surprised by the amount of wildlife.

"I'd think the environmentalists would be pretty happy about this." Around us fish were breaking the wind-rippled surface of the water and birds sat on the banks or flew overhead. Every hundred yards or so, we passed a crocodile sunning itself on the banks.

Although we wound through a dozen turns, it appeared as though we were following the only route to reach the site where I had seen the headlights. As we made a few more turns, it struck me again that whoever had dumped the body must have known the area. We got out of the UTV and scanned the ground. The storm had erased any sign of the tires tracks or any other evidence.

"There's nothing left."

6

Disappointed, we got into the UTV to head back. Bob skirted several potholes, then swerved to avoid a huge snake lying on the gravel road. "Damned pythons," he commented as he swerved around it. "Crocs are one thing, at least they're endangered. These Burmese Pythons are invasive."

The drive became monotonous. While Bob navigated through the maze of canals, I thought about how to handle Susan. We'd done this dance before and I knew she liked to lead. That was a problem for me. I was a lone wolf, both by my nature and how I had learned and preferred to work before. Back in California, I had patrolled close to ten thousand acres—alone. Now, living on Adam's Key, I handled the larger part of Biscayne Bay by myself.

This was not the first time Martinez had forced Susan on me. I looked back at her and noticed the same scowl on her makeup-hardened face that I probably had on mine. She didn't like this any better than I did.

The UTV came to a stop by the truck. We climbed out and thanked Bob for his help. He nodded and took off back in the direction of the security building. Standing there with Susan I decided the only thing to do was to take the high road.

"There's nothing left here. If there was anything besides the tire tracks, the storm wiped it out. Miami-Dade was able to take an imprint and pictures before the storm came in. We've got that lead and the autopsy."

"It's no secret that you're dating that forensics tech," she said. "Not that there's anything wrong with that."

I was pretty sure she had added the last part to cover the rumors floating around about her and Martinez. Trying to put aside the gruesome image of those two tangled together, I looked at my watch; it was still too early to contact Justine or Sid. They wouldn't be in for a few hours. "The activist group," I pulled out my notebook and scanned the two pages of notes. "MACE. We could check them out."

She actually almost smiled. "Now you're thinking. Motive in this case, is going to lead us to opportunity and means."

We climbed in the truck and left the plant. Again, I wondered about the lack of security for a nuclear facility. We left the landscaped property and passed the massive Homestead-Miami speedway. A glance over at Susan showed her typing into her phone.

"Their office is out by the Everglades. Keep going straight past the turnpike," she said.

I made my way west past the cluster housing and strip malls. Once we got beyond the turnpike, things started to change immediately. The suburban sprawl that had spread like a cancer from Miami ended and the area quickly turned agricultural. Planted fields lined the roads as far as I could see, which was a long way in the dead flat landscape. We came to a small town where Susan directed me to park. It was a downtown area like those in many small towns across the country. The buildings were mostly old and many needed repair, but it didn't look like there were many vacancies. The tone leaned to Hispanic.

"Should be over here," Susan said.

We approached an old brick storefront. The building had an old western facade that hid the plainness of a simple low-pitch gable roof. The door was recessed and definitely too small for wheelchairs.

As we squeezed through it, I wondered how it had escaped the ADA lawyers looking for an easy payday from non-compliant businesses.

We entered a large room with a half-dozen desks. All were cluttered with papers, which appeared to be flyers, brochures, press releases, and etc. Toward the back stood a pair of desks, one neat, the other stacked high with files. Behind the organized one sat a man who looked like he may have come with the building.

He got up and walked toward us before we could reach the desk. The tall ponytailed man held out a weathered hand.

"Amos Androssa."

I shook it, surprised by both the firmness of the grip and the intense gaze of his eyes. From the lines around them I guessed he was in his late sixties or early seventies. He eyed our uniforms.

"What can I do for our park service?" he asked.

It was hard to tell if he was friend or foe from the way he said it. There was a line in the sand between conservation and preservation, which the park service straddled uncomfortably. I needed to know which side he and his group were on. The debate was so intense in some areas that the park service had dedicated a webpage to define the two words. From my recollection, conservation sought the proper use of nature, a concept difficult to define. Preservation was more clear-cut. Its adherents sought the protection of nature from all human use. I was clearly on the conservation side and from my experience both fishermen and hunters, (with a few exceptions) took better care of the environment than the preservationists, who were after a utopia that was unachievable.

Forest fires in the west are a perfect example. An unmanaged forest often burned on its own to weed out the undergrowth and strengthen the remaining stock. Growth rings from sections of older trees often showed fires occurred several times in their life cycles. Extinguishing these natural events as well as eliminating logging, which as a byproduct, thinned the undergrowth, had proven to be detrimental to the environment. It was the preservation groups that had removed the wolves from Yellowstone and upset the natural balance there. In my view, nature left to its own devices worked. Yes, man's intervention needed to be minimal, thereby my conservationist view.

Looking at the eyes of the man standing across from me I knew from his hard look that he was a preservationist, though I had to admit, his ponytail played a part in that astute observation as well. Susan had picked up a brochure from one of the desks and before I could stop her she undercut my careful character assessment.

"Y'all can't decide what you want to do. Save the crocodiles or stop nuclear energy," she said.

"There's no reason you can't have both," Amos said, giving her a look that told me he could give a lecture at a moment's notice. "A shame about Edward. He was a promising young man."

We both nodded, though I had to look up slightly to meet his eyes. He had a way about him. Tall and lean, he naturally looked down on those he spoke to and his condescending tone didn't help; only confirming my original assessment was correct. "You heard?" I had expected we would break the news to him.

"Miami-Dade notified his parents last night. They are old friends of mine and called right away."

I guessed that old friends meant they were fellow activists and their son had been brought up with the hatred of man in his blood. "Any idea what he may have been working on?"

Susan handed me the brochure like I was an idiot. I already knew MACE wanted the Turkey Point plant closed. I just wanted Amos to say it.

"Edward was our attorney. He was involved in all our projects."

"We'd like a list of everything you've been working on for the past year," I said, thinking it would be a short list.

"It's all on our website. Unlike the government, we believe in transparency."

Susan already had her phone out. "These are all power plants. You want to shut down all of these?"

She handed me the phone. A quick glance showed at least a half-dozen targets in South Florida. There was a distressed look on her face.

"Do you want us back in the stone age?" she asked before I could stop her.

Her body language told me she was ready for a fight. Taking away her cell phone and lighted makeup mirror would be devastating to her, never mind the other inconveniences of a powerless world. I'd had my own run-ins with Amos's type out west. There was only fight. No discussions or conversation. You were wrong and they were right. These kinds of groups had learned since the sixties to use the media to cover their protests, making them seem larger than they were and then taking the matter to a carefully selected court that would use that same media bias to cover their tracks. They no longer cared about majority opinion. When you are right, that makes the other side wrong, regardless of how much they outnumber you.

"I'd like the opportunity to discuss our views with you," Amos said, smiling and looking directly at Susan.

I thought she swooned. In many cases I think it's funny how opposites attract. In this instance, not so much. I needed air. "I think that's all we have for you now. Just wanted to let you know about Edward," I said ushering Susan to the door. I watched the two of them eyeing each other as we left. She hastily scrawled something I suspected was her cell phone number on one of her cards and gave it to him with the standard, "if you think of something else" line. The door closed and we walked past several stores selling western boots and hardware. "You didn't need to start all that."

"Those people are dead wrong. That's not how you change things," she said.

It didn't matter that I agreed with her. I had carefully decided to disguise my views in the hope that Amos would open up and inadvertently give us a lead. All we had was a webpage, something we could have gotten without the drive here.

"Let's have a look at that website again," I said.

"I'm starving. Can we get something to eat?"

It was past noon and I was hungry too, but not going to admit it. "I suppose. There's a barbecue place across the street."

"Works for me," she said, crossing the two-lane road.

I waited for several pickups to pass before joining her, not failing to notice that the view from behind suggested that she could probably skip this meal. Catching up to her, I opened the door and we entered a different world from the one we had just left. This was salt of the earth. Picnic tables were set up in rows, crowded with the kind of people who wore blue jeans because they were functional, not stylish. They wore boots and plaid shirts. Smile lines highlighted their weathered faces.

We ordered and sat by a group of four men who appeared to be undeterred by our uniforms. Sipping iced teas, we waited for the food in the uneasy silence of people forced to be together. Susan pulled out her phone and started scanning through her Facebook feed. I tried to look away, but a notification popped up. Her text size was large, probably so she wouldn't have to succumb to wearing reading glasses. Before I could see any more, she turned her body.

It could still be work, I thought, though from the crack in her makeup when she smiled, I suspected otherwise. A few minutes later, our food was in front of us and she set the phone face down on the table. Eating allowed the silence to continue and with no conversation to get in the way, we finished in minutes.

Just as I put my fork down, my phone beeped. I picked it up and couldn't do anything about Susan's glance at the screen. My pre-forty eyes allowed me to size the text so she couldn't read it, which was a relief when I saw Justine's name on the screen. Even though I doubted she could make out the words, it was my turn to turn away. I texted back that I would call her later and turned back to the table.

"Ready?"

"Sure, where to now, boss?"

I had hoped to get rid of her, but that didn't look like it was happening. "From the look of things, FP&L probably had reason to want him dead."

"That's a pretty big corporation to arrest."

"Right, and a darned good red herring for someone else to throw out there. If they wanted him dead, they wouldn't do it on their own property. To me this has 'martyr' written all over it. We need to check out his friends."

"I'll go back and talk to Amos," Susan said.

I had no doubt she would.

7

I STOOD OUTSIDE THE RESTAURANT, pausing long enough to watch Susan saunter through the door of MACE headquarters. There was no talk about how she would get home, though I had a pretty good idea. Glad to be rid of her, I headed back to the turnpike and followed the signs to the northbound ramp and Miami. I thought as I drove, trying to piece the few clues I had into something that made sense. It was like a jigsaw puzzle; find the corners, fill in the borders, and the rest takes care of itself. So far, I had two corner pieces: FP&L and MACE, neither of which would do well with the publicity of a murder associated with them.

There are four corners to a puzzle and I knew there were more players involved. Things were never this simple. A jilted wife, ex, mother-in law, father-in law, even bitter kids. Statistics are clear that most murders are committed by someone known to the victim and often by a family member. Let Susan prod around old Amos's private parts. I was going to dig into Edward's family.

Before I delved into his lineage, I wanted to stop by the medical examiner's office to see if there was anything unusual about his death. It was still afternoon, and that likely meant Vance would be there. Sid's boss was also his protege, making for an interesting dynamic. The elder Jersey immigrant who preferred the night shift was getting ready to retire. Vance, the hipster wannabe fly fisherman was young enough to be his grandson, not that I'm one to judge, being only a few years older. Despite the small difference in age, I felt like we were from a different generation. Generation X and Y, Millennials—I could never get them straight. I think it was having kids that aged you in dog years, especially when you have them as young as Janet and I did. My daughter Allie would be fifteen soon and I realized it had been almost a year since the custody hearing that took her away from me. I missed her and wondered if it wasn't time to do something about that.

I exited the turnpike at the Don Shula expressway and followed that until turning east onto the 836. Coming from the backwoods of California, Miami traffic could only be described as interesting. Near the airport, the streets were crowded with trucks as well as low-riders, their subwoofers vibrating the entire road. Drivers were invisible here —behind heavily tinted windows. California required 88 percent of light to enter the front windows; Florida was only 28 percent. Mid-afternoon, the traffic was heavy but steady and I reached the NW 12th Ave exit a few minutes later. Following the signs to Jackson Memorial Hospital, I skirted the perimeter and turned into the large parking lot that serviced the tropically landscaped three building complex.

Vance was at work in the exam room, and though he waved me in, I declined, deciding to wait. I texted Justine to see if I could run by and see her when I was done here and got an emphatic yes with a smiley face. Dead bodies usually put her in a good mood. I thought Sid had completed the autopsy last night, but the body on the other side of the glass partition looked like Edward.

I knocked on the glass window and a minute later Vance came to the door. "Is that Edward?" I asked.

"Just having a look. Sid said there were some bites on his leg that he couldn't identify. Care to join me?"

I thought I had dodged that bullet last night and swallowed, checking the acid level in my stomach. Despite having to dine with Susan, lunch had digested well, and I decided to take a chance. "Sure, just give me a minute." I walked over to a rack of cubbies and put on a gown, cap, and mask. Taking a deep breath, I entered the room.

The sight of the body startled me. I had been present at two other autopsies, both involving floaters. Their corpses had been clinical; Edward was so close to a living human. Despite the Y incision in his chest, I half expected him to get off the table.

Clenching my gut, I walked closer. "Any sign of a struggle?" I asked, trying to break the ice.

"There's some bruising, definitely before he died. I scraped his fingernails to see if there is any forensic evidence."

He moved out of the way to allow me to see the wounds. The blood was coagulated and when he manipulated the knee joint to allow a better view, the muscle flexed. "When does rigor mortis set in?" I asked.

If he'd had reading glasses, it would have been the same look that Sid gave me when I said something stupid.

"We're into what we call the "passed" stage, when the muscles become flexible again," he said, factually.

Deciding I had better stop the questions and learn through observation, I watched him as he prodded and measured the wound. The flesh was torn and looked like a large animal had gotten him. He stepped away and retrieved a jar. Now, I almost gagged when I saw the dead man's lungs floating in embalming fluid. He looked at them carefully.

Sid said they were full of water. I would have thought the cause of death was the leg wound had bled out—but as usual, he's correct. I had watched enough CSI to know that lungs full of water meant that Edward had drowned.

"Cause of death is drowning," Vance said with finality and placed a sheet over the body. He pulled off his gloves, tossed them into a hazardous materials bin, and removed his facemask.

"Any idea about what could have done that to his leg? Maybe a gator?" There were attacks on the news all the time. I remembered the crocodiles sunning themselves on the banks of the cooling canals. Maybe one had found him in the water. "What about a crocodile?"

"You need a zoologist, not a medical examiner," he said.

"Can I get pictures?"

He walked over to his computer at his stand-up desk. A few minutes later, several eight-by-ten prints were in my hand. "Any luck with the bonefish?"

I knew that was coming. At our last meeting he had helped me out on my case and I had promised him a trip. "I'm onto a few spots. Still haven't got one to bite yet. I think we have to wait for the weather to settle." I had no problem with him knowing I was a novice. He'd find out soon enough when I took him out. I wondered how that bit of professional courtesy was going to go with Martinez. There was pretty much no way that situation was going to turn out well. Maybe if Vance played golf, but considering his "greased up" hair and manicured mustache, I couldn't see him in a polo shirt.

"Next week?"

"Let me get through this case and we'll hook up," I said, realizing the pun too late.

He laughed and shook my hand. My apprehensions about him were fading. At least he had a sense of humor. He would need that to fish with me. I left the office and headed outside. It was twilight now—Justine time—and I headed to the truck with the pictures in my hand and a smile on my face.

My next stop was the crime lab. Heading back onto the 836, I passed the airport and took the Palmetto Expressway, exiting onto NW 12th Ave. I made my way through the construction to the Miami-Dade Crime Lab lot and parked. I still had a smile plastered on my face and the pictures were still in hand when I entered the building and walked downstairs to the forensics lab.

I saw her before she saw me and I took a minute to watch her through the glass partition between the hall and the lab before entering. Only a hint of the great body I had recently discovered could be seen as she moved to the music I knew was blasting through her headphones. With her braided hair bouncing to the beat of the reggae, she turned.

"Hey, wanna check out the tire tracks?" she asked, placing the headphones around her neck.

The music was loud. She must have seen my face and reached for a knob. The volume receded to a level you would expect from headphones. "Sure, I just came from the medical examiner's office and have some stuff too." I proudly handed her the pictures, knowing they would get a more enthusiastic reception than tire tracks. Nothing turns a girl on like animal bites.

"Oh, this *is* cool," she took the pictures from my hand, studying them as she brought them to a table. "Gator?"

"Nope," I answered, trying not to be too smug. Score one for me. "I think they're American crocodile."

"Get out."

She gave me the same look as Sid and I wondered if they taught it at some forensics academy. "American crocodile," she said to herself, turning to a computer monitor. She must have seen my disappointment. "Trust but verify. I see a lot of gator bites here. You're right, this is narrower and the teeth are different."

She moved over, allowing me a look at the Wikipedia page for the American crocodile. I scanned the article, pausing on the sentence that said they didn't often attack larger animals. With Justine leaning over me, I went to Google and entered *American crocodile attacks*. There were few results and only one local case of a man in Coral Gables bitten by one while swimming in a canal.

"They don't usually attack humans," I pointed out.

She went to the monitor next to mine and started typing while I continued reading. It appeared the presentation at the power plant this morning was more truthful than the propaganda I took it for. The cooling canals at the Turkey Point plant were essential to the survival of the species in North America. The protected and warmed canals provided the ideal environment for the species to survive. Since the plant's inception in the seventies they had increased their population from only a few hundred to several thousand and were no longer on the endangered species list. They were now classified as threatened.

Another corner of the puzzle fell into place. MACE was looking at an impossible choice. By closing the plant, they would endanger the crocodiles; leaving it open was against their mandate. I wondered where Amos stood on this environmental Catch-22.

I looked over at Justine, focusing on her curves underneath the lab coat. A wave of excitement and also fatigue came over me. There was little I could accomplish until morning. "Want to get some dinner?"

Sitting in the restaurant down the street from the crime lab, I fought to stay off work related topics. That had been my downfall before and caused the two fights our fledgling relationship had survived. I asked about her training for a paddleboard race she was interested in. That took us until the food arrived. We ate in silence like an old couple comfortable with each other and when the check arrived, I took it and paid.

"My place?" she asked, handing me a key.

"You bet," I answered, taking my chit to a level five relationship.

8

It was still dark in the room when Justine kicked me awake. I thought she had just gotten home from work, and rolled over hoping to consummate the new level of our relationship, but she quickly hopped out of bed. It wasn't going to be. I watched her walk toward the bathroom with nothing on to hide her curves. Grabbing my phone from the nightstand, I saw it was seven o'clock already and the darkness was fabricated by her blackout shades. When you work nights, you do whatever you can to get sleep.

There were no messages and I pushed off the covers, regretting that I had slept through the night and not awakened when she got home. A minute later, as I rolled out of bed, she emerged from the bathroom with her hair in her standard tight braid and went for the closet. I got up, realizing the chance for anything I had in mind was gone and went for the bathroom. When I emerged, she was already dressed in khaki pants and a long sleeve shirt—way more clothes than I was used to seeing on her. The cold front that had blown through the other night had taken an edge off the humidity and knocked the daytime highs into the low seventies, but even for the tropically acclimated, I thought her overdressed.

I might have gotten a key, but I was still without my own drawer so I had to dress in the same uniform I had on yesterday. Fortunately, I had spent most of the day either inside or in the truck and the clothes had another day left in them. On a typical day, they would be unwearable.

"What's the plan?" I asked following her into the kitchen.

She made a pot of coffee and slugged down a large glass of water. She refilled it and handed it to me, waiting while I drank it. "Got to watch the hydration."

"Where are we going?"

"To meet Steve," she said, pouring the coffee into two stainless cups.

"Steve?"

"You'll love him. Come on, time to go to school," she said, giving me an alluring look on the way out the door.

I drove while she gave directions. We were heading west when she finally gave me my first clue.

"Ever been to the Everglades?"

I'd been near them, but not in them. "Just as far as Redlands."

"You're gonna love this."

That was all she was giving me as she directed me to exit the Turnpike and follow the signs for highway 41 west. With the rising sun in my rearview mirror, we gradually left civilization. The strip centers and housing developments ended. Sawgrass stretched for as far as I could see on the left, broken occasionally by an oasis of cypress trees. On the right ran a wide canal with cars parked off to the side. Groups of people were sitting in lawn chairs and fishing with cane poles. We had clearly left Miami. After we passed Krome Avenue, Justine got out her phone and texted someone. A minute later her phone chimed and she directed me to a pullout on the right.

I parked near an airboat that was pulled onto a small beach created by the road spoils. A man dressed the same as Justine walked toward us. We exited the truck and met him halfway between the boat and the truck. Looking like triplets in our khakis, Justine hugged him and introduced me to Steve.

"He's a zoologist," she said.

Without a word, he handed us ear protection and advised us to put on sunglasses if we had them. Once we were ready and seated side-by-side in the front of the airboat, he climbed onto the driver's seat perched a foot or so above us and started the engine. The aircraft engine roared to life and I knew why we needed the ear protection.

As he swung the flat bow around, I was expecting a boring nature lesson. What I got was as exhilarating as a ride in any amusement park. Cruising at what I guessed was close to fifty mph, I found out why he recommended sunglasses as he veered out of the main channel and entered a smaller one. The low flat bow of the airboat snapped the cattails in our path, launching their tops at our faces. I could imagine him grinning in his seat a few feet above us as he turned hard to the left. I was almost thrown from my seat when the boat angled into the turn and reached for the seatbelt that he had neglected to include in his two-sentence safety briefing. We entered an even smaller channel and I could feel the boat slow and turn again into a small cove, where we came to a stop. Steve cut the engine.

The silence was overwhelming at first. Slowly I regained my hearing and noticed the sounds of birds and other animals in the background. Justine smiled next to me and Steve let us have a minute to be with nature in a way not many experience.

"They love Cheetos," he said, tossing a handful into the water.

I wasn't sure who the *they* he was referring to were. Justine was alert and scanning the water when I heard a low guttural groan. I looked around and realized it was Steve. Before I could ask what he was doing, something moved to our right and a gator emerged from the cover of the sawgrass.

Steve tossed a few more Cheetos at the snout and I watched it open slowly, revealing rows of razor sharp teeth.

"Gator has a wider snout than the crocodile. Grow bigger too. This one's a female, and about six feet. Her mate's around here somewhere." He grunted again.

This time it was returned by another and the three of them were soon engaged in some kind of prehistoric conversation. A minute later the sawgrass parted and the female took off. I followed her wake until it was gone and turned to the new visitor. I guessed from his size that this was the mate that Steve was referring to. An easy twelve feet, he was clearly more aggressive than the female. Raising his snout out of the water, he opened his mouth and waited.

"We get to know each other after a while," Steve said, tossing a handful of Cheetos into the waiting jaws. "Not that he wouldn't have you for lunch."

"What's the difference between these guys and the crocodiles?"

"To start with they're from different families. Gators are aggressive. They're opportunistic eaters and often resort to cannibalism. The American crocodile is generally much more sedate, though they can be aggressive as well. They'll grow to about the same sizes, but being saltwater acclimated, subsist mainly on fish and aquatic creatures. It's pretty rare to see them attack a mammal of any kind."

"So a body thrown into the cooling canals down at Turkey Point wouldn't be fair game?"

He shook his head and tossed another handful of Cheetos onto the water. The gator looked like a log with just the top of its head exposed. I had almost forgotten it was there when it snapped at the corn chips floating its way.

"That population is thriving. No one fishes those canals so there's plenty of food. Probably get the stray turtle or bird too. Unless it attacked first, I doubt they would mess with it."

"Why then? The medical examiner says the victim was probably unconscious when he was thrown in the water."

I looked at the stream of floating corn chips and watched the gator snap at the closest. It gave me an idea. "What if it was baited?"

He shrugged like this was the dumbest thing he'd ever heard. I continued anyway. "You know, if there were fish or something the crocodile would be attracted to the body?"

"Might work. Especially around sunrise or sunset when they are actively feeding," Steve said.

"It was sunset," I said. "I was on the other side of the embankment, so I didn't see what happened in the water."

"That'd be a pretty trick way of killing someone without murdering them yourself," Justine said.

I thought about that for a second; unsure how using bait to get an animal to kill someone worked with homicide. Before I could come to a conclusion, my phone vibrated in my pocket. Surprised that there was service out here, I pulled it from my pocket, already suspecting who it was. Martinez's name appeared on the screen with a question: *What the hell are you doing in the Everglades?*

There was no escaping his tracking methods. I knew he watched his agents through GPS trackers in the park service boats and vehicles. He also had an eye in the sky that knew where I was by my phone's location. "Crap," I muttered.

"That your boss?"

Justine must have heard me. "Yeah."

Before I could answer, another text came in, this time from Susan saying she had found something and asked where I was. I doubted that she needed an answer to the second part, expecting her to be in Martinez's office working some well-orchestrated plot to entrap me. I shut the power off to the phone, knowing they could still track me. "Let's keep going," I said. After all, it was research and I might never get this chance again.

Steve fired up the engine and we watched as the gator spun and headed for cover. A few minutes later, we were back to full speed. With the tops of the beheaded cattails slapping my face I reached over for Justine's hand. I looked over at her and saw the smile on her face. Whatever I had to face from headquarters, it was worth this.

Steve steered a circular course that took us around several of the small islands I had seen from the road before returning to the small beach by the highway. We said our goodbyes and exchanged contact info. When we got back to the truck, I thanked Justine and checked my phone.

Several messages waited. Two from Martinez and one from Susan. His were the usual, hers was more intriguing and I was just about to dial her number when two voicemails came through.

"Your girlfriends are all looking for you," Justine teased, leaning over my shoulder.

We were close together and she could easily see the screen of my phone. I was on the spot now, and regardless of who the calls were from, if they were business, I would usually listen to them privately. Now, with Grace Herrera and Rebecca Moore's names on the screen I couldn't save them for later with Justine looking on. Even though I had a key to her apartment in my pocket, we were too new at this for me to have her full trust.

"You going to check those or stare at me like you're doing something wrong?" she asked and smacked me on the arm.

With things seemingly back to normal, I got into the truck on the driver's side, removed my pad and pen from my pocket and with the phone on my lap retrieved the messages. I felt surrounded by women with Justine next to me, awaiting voicemails from two others, and Susan McLeash trying to track me down. Even Martinez would be a welcome reprieve from the estrogen.

I placed the phone on speaker and retrieved Grace's message first. Being a Miami-Dade officer gave her priority.

"Got the cause of death from the coroner and wanted to talk to you about it. Also have some info on the deceased. Call when you can."

That one was almost too easy. There wasn't a hint of anything but business. Hoping Rebecca's would be similar, I retrieved hers next.

"Hi, there Kurt," the message started.

From the tone of her voice I knew I was in trouble.

"You asked me to call if I remembered anything and I have. It might not be important, but maybe we could meet for a drink later and discuss it."

This couldn't have sounded any worse, especially since Justine wasn't at the meeting yesterday. Even to my naive ears it was an invitation to more than a conversation.

"Hmm," Justine started. "I've got some information for you too. Maybe we could talk about it in bed."

I breathed a sigh of relief after hearing her tone. She was surrounded by men at work who constantly hit on her. I had seen it firsthand and asked her why she didn't report it. Her answer was that her career would be ruined even if she were proven to be truthful. In a male dominated police force, a woman had to be careful. She had reassured me that it had never gone past what ten years ago we would have called playful banter.

I trusted her and I was glad when she returned it. I made note of both numbers, put the pad back in my pocket, and pressed the icon for the favorites screen. It had not been my choice to put him there, but the park service phone had come programmed with several numbers, Martinez's being one of them.

"The Everglades? What the hell, Hunter?"

"I'm on my way in. I'll explain when I get there."

9

I STOOD in the doorway waiting for Martinez to finish his phone call. It often happened this way; me standing there while he gave urgent orders that I suspected were to imaginary callers. While I waited I looked around his office noticing the row of generic looking golf trophies on the credenza behind his desk and wondered if they were no more real than the imaginary callers.

Finally, he put down the phone and motioned me to a chair.

"Progress?" he asked without preamble.

"Yes." I hoped to leave my report at one word.

"Go on."

"Susan and I have talked to the FP&L people. The victim, Edward Ingerman was an attorney for an environmental activist group called the Miami Alliance for Clean Energy or MACE. There seems to be a divide in the group between saving the crocodiles or closing the plant. Susan interviewed the founder yesterday."

"I know, she at least files reports," he snipped. "What was so important out in the Everglades this morning?"

I had forgotten for a second that he knew where I had been. My phone rang saving me from an explanation that he wouldn't buy. Telling Martinez my latest hunch about baiting the body to attract the crocodile which would then actually commit the murder was not going to get me an atta-boy. I looked at the screen and saw Grace Herrera's name.

"Mind if I take this? It's the Miami-Dade detective."

He nodded. Although we were a federal agency, we relied heavily on the locals for support. I thought about turning away, but I had nothing to hide.

"Hi, Grace," I answered.

"Hard to get ahold of you," she said. "Just a heads up that there is going to be a protest at the Turkey Point plant later today. The murder hit the papers this morning and roused up every activist in town."

"I'll be there," I said and we agreed on a time and place to meet.

Martinez looked away from the dual monitors on the side of his desk that he used to oversee the park. "What's Miami-Dade want with you?"

I guessed there was no harm in telling him. It was okay to use them, but when they needed something of us, it was a burden on his budget. He didn't get the "quo" part of quid pro quo. "Protest at the power plant later today."

"Crocodiles and protests are not going to close this case. Find something on that Amos guy and end this."

It was Susan's words coming out of his mouth. This was more complicated than that and we both knew it. He was just hoping for a happy ending and an appearance on the five o'clock news, maybe the six if things dragged. Then back to grinding on his agents to make his reports look good.

"Right. I'll check in with you later," I said, knowing I wouldn't.

He dismissed me with his eyes and I quickly left the office. Looking at my watch, I saw it was already noon. With a rumbling stomach and a few hours to kill before the protest, I decided to head home and get a change of clothes and something to eat. The baiting idea was eating at me and there was also a fishing guide that I hoped to run into on the way who might be able to shed some light.

The twenty-two-foot center console seemed sluggish and slow as it got up on plane. Powered by a single outboard, it was nothing like the power of the engine pushing the ultralight airboat. I enjoyed it anyway. With my phone in the console and the roar of the engine muting it and any other sound, I was free at least for the twenty-minute ride out to Adams Key.

Reaching the dock, I noticed the tide running through the cut and slowed to go bow in. Fifty feet out, I set out the fenders, readied the lines, and nosed forward. When the bow was six feet away from the dock, I dropped into neutral and ran forward reaching the bow just as it touched the concrete. In the past, I had scarred the hull with my novice attempts at docking. Now, with a little practice I was good enough that I hadn't alerted Zero.

I tied off the bow line, then waited for the tide to push the stern back against the dock before securing the boat. I looked around at the conditions. There was no need for a spring line. Roy's boat was gone and I wouldn't be here long enough to worry about it. Just as I turned to the house, I heard the crash of the screen door and there was Zero, barreling toward me. With his heavy build and low center of gravity, the white pit bull mix with the brindle patch over his eye reminded me of Petey from the Little Rascals. When he ran, he looked like a rolling bowling ball. He skidded to a stop by my side, panting hard. I scratched his ears and heard the door slam again.

Becky came toward me with Jamie on her hip and I knew I would have to answer for last night's absence. Mariposa and Becky were the coconut telegraph for the park; what one didn't know the other did.

"How's that new girlfriend of yours doing?" she asked.

"It's all good," I said.

"You oughta bring her 'round for some yellowtail one of these days. Sure'd be nice to get to know her."

I guessed she had been talking to Mariposa and knew about our plans. Except for the interrogations that were bound to happen, both offers were hard to refuse.

"You got it. Once this case is done, I'll bring her out."

"Heard you got another floater."

"Seem to find me I guess."

"You know what they say," she said, laughing to herself.

That one could go either way so I left it alone. "Want me to watch Zero for a while? I'll only be here an hour or so." If there was one way to win favor with Becky, it was to take Zero off her hands. With only our two residences on the island you'd think it would be quiet. Some days it is, but others, between the traffic at the day-use area and Caesars Pass, Zero had a full day of barking.

"Appreciate that," she said. "I'll go put the young'un down for his nap and bring you some snapper."

"That'd be great," I said, starting to turn away. "Hey, have you seen Chico come through today?"

"Not yet. Could've missed him. Tide's running hard now. If he's got a charter I'd expect to see him soon."

Chico was one of the local fishing guides. There were a half-dozen pros that frequented the park and I had gotten to know most of them. Many were standoffish and stayed to themselves; Chico was willing to offer advice to a novice. Not surprisingly, he was also the busiest. I looked back at the cut and channel into Jones Lagoon. There was no sign of Chico's aqua bottomed flats boat. I turned with Zero on my heels to go inside.

After a quick shower, I checked my phone. There was a text from Justine and a missed call from Rebecca Moore. I realized I had forgotten to call her back and hit her name on the screen.

"Well hey, sunshine," she answered.

I had a feeling this was not going to be all business. To my relief, I heard a knock on the door. With the phone in hand, I went to answer. Becky stood there with a plate full of fried snapper, hushpuppies, and a buttered piece of cornbread. Alabama gulf coast cooking at its finest.

"Saw Chico head up into the mangroves on the way over," she said, handing me the food.

"Thanks," I said. "I have to head out in a few."

"Come on, boy," Becky called. "Time to do your job and keep the young'un company." Zero's ears perked up somehow knowing we were talking about him. He followed her out the door, casting a look back at me that said he'd rather stay and sleep all afternoon in peace. It wasn't until the door closed behind them that I heard a voice on the line.

"If I'm interrupting?"

I could hear the lawyer tone in her voice. It was a fine line I had to walk. Her apparent interest in me could work to my advantage. In most cases, I wouldn't think this way, but dealing with a lawyer the decision was easy. Had the tables been turned, she would do the same. "No, my neighbor just brought over a plate of food." It was always best to tell the truth.

"I thought you lived out on one of those deserted islands?"

"There're two houses. Ray, the maintenance guy, and his family live in the other."

"Oh. So, I got a call from Officer Herrera this morning that there is going to be a protest here this afternoon. I've heard that murderers like to revisit the scene of their crimes. This might be the perfect opportunity."

"I heard that too. I was planning on heading over soon. Can I dock anywhere by the plant or do I need to go and get a vehicle?"

"There's a marked channel just to the north of Turkey Point with a small dock. I'll meet you there."

I decided on easy instead of smart. "I can be there in about an hour."

"Great," she said and hung up.

I stared at the phone like I had done something wrong and then remembered Justine's text. I pecked out a quick message that I was going to find Chico and then head over to the protest. I would check in later. There was no fast reply, which wasn't unusual. It was after three now and I could see her ensconced in her headphones with her braid bopping to whatever beat she was listening to.

I pulled my pistol from the drawer where I left it when I was home and inspected if carefully. Small, pitted spots were already appearing where the salt had eaten through the last coating of oil. The ocean environment was hard on anything mechanical, and I knew it needed to be cleaned. Deciding that finding Chico was more important, I placed it in my holster and left the house.

The tide was really moving now and I had to think about how to depart the dock. Only the fenders kept the boat from slamming into the structure with each passing wave. Reversing the process I had used earlier, I started the engine, released the bow line and let the current swing the front of the boat into the channel. Once it was clear, I released the stern line that had acted as a pivot point and motored slowly into the channel.

Following Caesars Creek to the ocean side, I passed the tip of Elliott Key and saw the aqua bottomed flats boat sitting behind the mangroves at Christmas Point. Chico stood on the poling platform with a long fiberglass pole in his hands. A lot of guides and anglers had switched to remote controlled battery-operated trolling motors and Power-poles. Chico was old school. He alternated between using the pole to push the boat forward and to point where he wanted the two anglers with him to cast. When he needed to anchor, he stuck the pole through a fitting on the gunwale into the bottom.

I kept my distance, unsure if this was a good or bad idea. Chico had taken me under his wing, showing me where to go and on what stage of the tide I would have the best shot at the bay's fish. He had schooled me on knots, flies, and rigging, all without asking anything in return.

"Hey, Kurt," he called over.

"I have a few questions, but don't want to spook the fish," I called back.

"They're not biting. We're going to move back into the lagoon." He hopped down from the platform making a thud on the deck, a move he never would have done if there were fish around. At the helm, he instructed his clients to stow their rods, started the engine, and motored toward me.

The look on the two men's faces was priceless as they stashed their beers and pulled out their wallets. "I'm not Fish and Game, no worries. Just have a question for Chico."

We pulled alongside each other and I reached over to grab his forearm. Holding the boats together with our grasp, I knew I only had a minute. "You know anything about scenting flies?" I asked.

The look on his face told me I had crossed a line. The two men perked up and I realized I had opened the Pandora's box of fly fishing. Generally, a purist sport, there were those out there that doped their flies, especially with certain species. "No, not you," I said. "A croc took a floater the other night near the cooling canals over at Turkey Point." The two men were interested now and moved closer.

"I heard about that. Unusual for a croc to go after something that large."

"Right. Mostly they eat fish and reptiles. I was thinking the body might have been scented to attract it."

"Not my deal," Chico released my arm.

I knew he wanted to cut his losses and end the discussion. "No worries. Good luck."

He waved back at me as the boats drifted apart and I hoped I hadn't put him on the spot with his clients. Just before we were out of earshot the heavier of the two men yelled across at me.

"Menhaden oil. We use it for chum all the time."

"Thanks," I yelled, not knowing if he heard it over the roar of the engine as Chico sped away.

10

Hunters and fishermen have been aware of the power of scent for years. In general, the prey we seek has a much better sense of smell than we do—sometimes a hundred times greater. I'd done my share of hunting and knew how important it was to stay downwind and not allow my human scent to reach the deer, turkey, and feral pigs I had sought. I hunted the same way I fished, by trying to stalk my game. Many hunters preferred stationary blinds, where they could remain concealed until the game found them. Some were known to use bait to lure their prey closer. I had called in several sightings to the California Fish and Game when I had seen evidence of the dead carcasses of small animals, or a trail of blood or feed leading to a trampled-down area where I suspected a tree stand had been erected. Out west, this was very common when bear hunting. It works so well it is illegal in most places. I'd read about the same tactic being used for alligators here. Hanging a chicken from a low branch with a large hook embedded in it was a sure-fire way to bag a gator, but also illegal. Here, I had made several calls to the FWC after seeing suspect behavior.

    I remembered the slimy feel and off-scent of Edward when we pulled him from the water and it was still there later when Vance had removed the sheet to inspect the wounds. If the body had been in the water longer, the scent would have worn off, and the green slime that covers anything submerged in tropical seas would appear, disguising the applied scent. Having found the body so quickly had subverted that, possibly giving us a big clue.

Thinking about this on the way to Turkey Point, I decided to send a couple of inquiries: one to Vance at the medical examiner's office and the other to a friend who worked for the FWC. I hoped Vance could confirm the presence of a foreign substance on the corpse and if so, I would be able to get a general sense of whether my idea would work, and Pete Robinson at FWC could give me his first hand take on whether this had been done before.

I approached the small cove with the email composed in my head, ready to enter and send it from my phone as soon as I tied off. That plan fell apart when I saw Rebecca already waiting for me on the dock. She motioned to me and I tossed her the bow line while I dropped the fenders over and eased the boat to the dock. Her heel caught in the gap between the deck-boards and she lost her balance. I don't know if there is a proper way to dress for a protest, but I was pretty sure that what she was wearing was not it. Her short skirt rode high on her thighs and I couldn't help but gape at the cleavage visible when she tripped. The email slipped from my mind and I smiled awkwardly at her.

"Hey, sailor," she called after retreating to more solid ground.

It was a graceful recovery, and I finished securing the boat before joining her. If you asked Susan, it was probably against regulations, but while onboard, I preferred to leave my gun belt in the watertight glove compartment rather than wear it. There is usually plenty of time to retrieve it if I have an encounter on the water, and the weapon is protected from the elements. I opened the compartment and slid the webbed belt around my waist, reasoning that this was an official visit and I was on a case. Secondary in my mind was that I might need it to fight off Rebecca, who clearly approved of the weapon.

"Ms. Moore," I answered, hoping to keep this official.

"Oh, please. My friends call me Becky."

I guess there was no choice then. "Okay, hey, Becky." This brought another sheepish smile to her face. She stood there in what was essentially a cocktail dress and high heels. Same look, different day. "Has the rally started yet?"

"They're starting to gather," she said, motioning to another of the four-wheel drive UTVs the company used to get around the property. "Got to run by the office first and change. I was running late from a meeting and didn't want to miss you."

I had totally misread that situation and silently scolded myself. My ego took a small hit and my investigative skills a larger one as we drove to the main office building where we'd had the meeting yesterday. The email suddenly reappeared in my head, and when we got there, she deposited me in a comfortable chair in the lobby where, under the watchful eyes of the receptionist, I pecked out my request and pressed send. The swoosh sound notified me that the email was in the ether and then I thought it might have been a good idea to copy Susan and Martinez. At least let them know I was out there. I forwarded the message to both of them, pecked out a quick hello to Justine, and sat back to wait for Rebecca.

She appeared again, looking like she had planned her outfit to the last detail. Looking at her, I decided that my first reaction had been correct; she dressed for maximum exposure. Dressed in tight-fitting jeans and a blouse that looked like it had come from an outdoors store. With the sleeves rolled up and the top few buttons carefully left undone, she nodded to me and we went back to the UTV. I glanced over at her as we drove. Gone was the barroom floozy and in her place was some kind of outdoor sexy seductress. Turning away to avoid going blind, I looked ahead to the group of people in front of the entry to the canals.

The cooling canal area was only slightly more secure than the rest of the property. The access roads were gated with a yellow version of the standard park service gate. The only areas I had seen with the same security measures were the high-voltage transmission lines. Standing in the bed of a UTV with a bullhorn in his hands was Bob, the guard who had given me the tour earlier. Even from where we sat, well behind the crowd, I could hear his pleas for them to disperse.

Not dispersing only gave the hundred or so protesters something to agree on. In two separate groups with the road dividing them, the two factions looked the same,

"Look at them. This is great. They're eating each other alive," Rebecca said.

The excited smile I had thought reserved for me was back and I scanned the crowd. By nature, a protest requires two diametrically opposed ideas. The notable images that come to mind are hippies versus the establishment, and the civil rights color-versus-color marches. I started to study them, trying to pinpoint what Rebecca was talking about when a TV van pulled up.

The doors opened at once and three people exited the van. In what could have been a choreographed dance, the satellite antenna was cranked up, the talent checked her makeup, and the director and video guys surrounded her in seconds with a portable mixing board and a camera. They moved quickly into the divide between the groups and I tried to see the protest through the camera's eyes. Rebecca fluffed her hair at the sight of them.

The only difference between the groups were the signs they carried: *Save the Crocodiles* on one side and *Shut Down the Plant* on the other. Under normal circumstances they would have seemed complementary views; in this case they were contradictory. The crocodiles needed the warm water from the plant to survive: no plant, no crocodiles. I looked over at Rebecca, who stood next to me watching the crowd with a smile on her face that suggested she was proud of something. She saw the TV crew start pulling people from the crowd for the ten-second sound bites that fueled their broadcasts. "Gotta go to work," she said, checking her face and hair in a small mirror.

She climbed out of the UTV and walked over to the news crew. Seconds after introducing herself to the director she was standing next to the reporter with the camera focused on her. I was curious to see how she was going to spin this, so I got out and wandered within earshot.

She was good. Spinning the story about FP&L caring about both groups concerned. The crocodiles were a slam-dunk for her. The plant could operate as it had since the seventies with its man-made environment nurturing the endangered reptiles. The opposition to the plant in general was a little tougher, but I gave her good grades on what sounded like a well-practiced speech about FP&L meeting or beating all the deadlines to clean up the canals. What she didn't mention, and what I had found on the first page of Google, was that the cleanup had been mandated by several government agencies.

A tall figure emerged from one side and approached the news crew. It was Amos, standing almost a head taller than the crowd. Behind him, I was surprised to see Susan McLeash.

I don't have much of a stomach for politics. I vote my heart and mind; not some party line dictated by people like Rebecca Moore. As little as I knew about it, I did know suicide when it was about to happen, and pushed through the crowd trying to reach Susan before the cameras saw her in her park service uniform. It might have been all right for Martinez to get in front of the cameras, and I glanced around the crowd half expecting to see him. For Susan, this was a no-win.

Reaching her at the edge of the crowd, I pulled her aside. "What are you doing?"

"I was going to see if they have any questions, and give a statement about the investigation."

"That's not why they're here. They smell blood in the water between these two groups. The murder might have been the catalyst for this, but this is not about Edward."

She pulled against my grasp, seeing her fifteen minutes of fame standing twenty feet from her. "Why do you have to be a buzz-kill about everything?"

I had no choice but to let her go, but I did have one card left. "Does Martinez know you are doing this? Giving a statement?"

That got her attention. She turned back to me with the scowl of a two-year-old. "It's what he'd do," she said defensively, but joined me at the edge of the crowd.

I was about to ask her what she was doing with Amos when the two groups started moving toward one another. There were three TV vans now, their crews circulating between Amos, Rebecca, and whoever they could snag from the crowd. They all scattered when the crowd started to close around them.

The protest was quickly turning into a riot. Over by the fence, Bob stood in the bed of his UTV with his bullhorn totally ineffective over the ruckus. When Amos reached the front of one group, a tall woman emerged from the other. Something looked familiar about her. She was tall and lean with her hair tied back in a ponytail. She strode directly toward Amos and I could immediately see the resemblance —they were brother and sister, possibly twins.

Behind them, the crowds seemed to compress as the two environmentalists converged. The buzz of the protest seemed to increase. I thought Susan said something. I tapped my ear to indicate I couldn't hear her.

"Who is that?"

"I don't know, but they look like twins."

"Duh, didn't you run a background check on him?" she asked.

I looked back at her. "You were the one with him. My job was to handle the coroner and forensics if I remember correctly." That shut her down and she turned away and started typing into her phone. Amos and the other woman were toe-to-toe now, shouting insults in each other's faces. The groups behind them caught the buzzwords and chanted them as if following along with a preacher at Sunday services.

"It's his sister," Susan yelled.

She held out her phone and I read the Wikipedia page. Adrian and Amos Androssa were indeed siblings. There was some background, including notes that each had been arrested several times. As I was reading, I heard a loud crash, but when I looked for the source, all I could see were the crowds surging forward. It appeared the siblings' criminal records would need to be amended shortly.

The crowd jostled us about and a fight broke out. This was going sideways and I looked around for a way to break it up when a gunshot sounded close by. It quieted the crowd immediately and they started to retreat when another shot was fired. It was close to my ear, so close that it could have been me that shot it. I turned to look for the source and found Susan standing next to me with my gun in her hand and a smile on her face.

I grabbed the weapon from her, holstered it, making sure to secure the strap and scanned the crowd. The protesters were starting to disperse. The two instigators, both visible over the heads of the others were smiling. An unusual reaction to what I thought was a botched protest.

11

"What do you mean she took your gun and fired it?" Martinez screamed.

We were sitting in his office. On my way in Mariposa had warned me that he already knew what had happened. That didn't surprise me, he'd probably watched the whole thing live on TV.

"We were jostled by the crowd. She must have pulled it from my holster and fired." I couldn't tell from his expression which way this was going to go, but I should have known.

"You fired your own gun. That's how the report you're about to write is going to read." He must have seen the look on my face. "Don't take it so badly. The gunshots broke up a riot. Maybe you'll make the news," he said with a smirk.

He had no interest in me getting credit for anything; it was all about Susan getting a pass for her actions. Already on probation, taking my weapon and firing it would have gotten her suspended at the least. There was an even better chance that she would lose her job. I only had seconds to decide if I was going to cooperate and I realized that it was, after all, my gun. If her fingerprints were on it, they would have been smudged when I grabbed the gun from her.

Unless someone had caught it on video the only other way to implicate her was if there was gunshot residue on her hands but she knew how to erase that.

"Okay, I'll cover for her."

"That'a boy, Hunter. It's beginning to feel like a team around here."

I nodded and left his office wondering what glue he was sniffing. At least I could call the score settled between Susan and me. I had to trust that Martinez would do his part and rubber-stamp my report. Heading to my cubby hole of an office, I saw Susan enter Martinez's lair and wished I could have been a fly on the wall. Call me paranoid, but I was seeing setups all around me. First Adrian and Amos at the rally, and now Susan and Martinez.

Discharging a weapon required a report. Sitting at my desk, I started to work up the alleged circumstances that led to me firing two shots. Once I had the paperwork complete, I emailed it to Martinez and sat back, staring at my unadorned walls wondering what to do next.

The image of Adrian and Amos smiling at each other when the rally broke up came back to me, and I turned to my computer and opened a browser window. Dodging the urge to go into the park service's password-encrypted database and trying to find the report Susan had written that had resulted in her probation, I typed in *Adrian Androssa*. The results were similar to the search I had done on Amos. I clicked through, determined that the same Wikipedia page that Susan had shown me was the most complete, returned to it, and read it more carefully. It could have been a duplicate of Amos's. Further increasing my suspicion was an address of her office at the bottom. It was in Redland, and I confirmed it by opening another window and checking Amos's page. The two were the same.

I'd had enough of the office for one day and decided to make a late afternoon visit to Redland. They would hardly be expecting me, probably thinking I was in some kind of hearing after Susan fired my weapon. That could be what they were smiling about—the downfall of any law enforcement officer or agency was always on top of most activists' agendas. It didn't seem to matter that the park service protected the parks; they wanted them closed to the public.

Mariposa didn't have quite the same hold on me now that I had my own truck and keys, but I still stopped by whenever I passed her desk. She knew more about what was going on here than Martinez.

"Hey, Kurt Hunter. I have a chicken already in the pot for dinner tomorrow night. You and that pretty girl of yours come over at seven." She handed me her address already written on a piece of paper. I accepted the ambush graciously, thinking it would be a good break and that her husband would be appreciative, finally being able to drink the "guest only" rum.

"You got it."

Her smile could light a room. "It'd be about time."

"I gotta go follow some leads," I said.

She motioned me closer. "Watch that Susan McLeash."

I took the advice to heart and left the building. It was close to five now and I hoped I would find the twins watching the news in their shared office while toasting their victory. Traffic was light heading to the Turnpike, but in the eastbound lane there was a string of large trailers heading towards me. They were enclosed, but the graphics said *race car* all over them. Each one had the driver's picture and number on the side. I suspected that by later tonight there would be a long line of RVs following the same path. It looked like a busy weekend was coming up at Homestead-Miami Speedway.

Avoiding the Turnpike, I made my way to Redlands and parked down the street from the MACE office. It was close to six now and the winter sun was almost below the horizon. Lights were on in the open storefronts and I could see the activist office was illuminated. Now that I was here, I wasn't sure what to do until I spotted a bait and tackle store across the street. When all else fails....

The store had a wooden floor and an earthy feel similar to those in California. Out here, most of the merchandise was geared toward freshwater fishing. Several species of bass, gar, and other fish were prominent in the canals close by. A little further in, Everglades City had a small charter fleet and access to the upper parts of Florida Bay. Scanning the shelves, trying to figure out an angle to approach Adrian and Amos, I noticed a few bottles of chartreuse Fire Brine. It was common out west for salmon and steelhead, and I had to wonder what it was used for here. That brought me back to the menhaden oil.

The clerk looked up as I approached the register. I noticed he had been counting the cash drawer and was about to close. The grumpy look on his face turned sour when he noticed my uniform.

"I'm not from FWC," I said, holding my hands up in a peace offering.

"Park service though."

I realized we were on the border of the Everglades National Park. From what I'd heard, that was an entirely different gig from Biscayne Bay. Only a small fraction of the people using the bay were up to no good. The ratio was reversed in the Everglades where poaching and meth labs flourished. "I work Biscayne," I told him, smiling to ease the tension. Finally, he relaxed.

"Long way from the salt," he said.

"I'm here on some other business. Curious about a couple of things though." The look on his face told me I could continue but was on shaky ground. "What can you tell me about menhaden oil?"

"Good as it gets for chum and scent. 'Bout anything out there will react to it. Mixes with oats and sand, too."

I had seen bags of oats aboard some of the fishing boats in the bay and knew they used it for snapper. I guessed the oil was the secret sauce. "What about gators?" I asked, figuring out here he was more familiar with them than crocodiles.

"You sure you don't work the glades?"

"Really." It was time for a dose of the truth or I knew he'd shut down. "Fact is we had a floater in the bay that had a strange scent. Had bite marks we ID'd as being from a crocodile."

"Now that's curious. Just a rumor now, but I've heard that some of them poachers out in the glades've been scenting chickens and such trying to bait the gators."

"So it works then? I'd like to buy a bottle and play around with it." I pulled out my wallet and saw I had his attention.

"Now that stuff there," he pointed to the shelves. "That's all good, so far as it goes, but I got this secret brew." He stepped behind a partition, grabbed something from a rack concealed from the public, and set an unmarked gallon bottle on the counter. "It's a little pricey, but I guarantee results."

I pulled out my credit card.

"Sorry, son, just cash here."

Not only was the secret sauce secret, but the books probably were too. I pulled out two twenties and handed them over. Normally I would ask for a receipt and at least try to get reimbursed, but there was no chance of that here. Dismissing me, the clerk went back to counting the cash drawer. On my way out the door, I could see the light was still on in the MACE window and got an idea.

I turned back to the man, who gave me the *what now* look. "Those folks across the street, you have any dealings with them?"

"MACE? We don't exactly see eye to eye."

"I didn't expect you did. There was some action down at the Turkey Point power plant with them today."

"Saw that on the news. What are you wanting to know?"

"Do they ever come in here?"

"Not usually. Stream of hippies are in and out of their place though."

I had already figured that out. "What about unusually?"

"A woman came in last week asking about scent and stuff, just like you. She was a looker too."

I could see his face light up. My grandparents called this *schadenfreude*, German for the pleasure derived at another person's misfortune. I could see him get excited as he connected the dots. "Sold her two gallons of that same stuff."

I should have asked the question sooner and saved my forty dollars. I knew it was pointless to ask if there was a record of the transaction. It was another long shot, but I looked around to see if there were any security cameras. There were none visible.

"I appreciate your help," I said, walking toward the door.

"Anytime, old buddy," he called after me.

I stood on the sidewalk holding the unmarked gallon jug and realized it might not look good for a park service agent in uniform to be seen with it. Likely, many of the passersby knew what it was. I walked back to the truck and placed it inside, then went back to the MACE office.

Somehow, I had missed them. The lights were off and the door was locked. I looked around, and not seeing them on the streets, started walking back to my truck. Just before I got in, a Jeep passed by and I saw Adrian at the wheel. I quickly hopped in the truck, and without asking myself why, I pulled out and followed her.

The tail lights of the Jeep were just visible when I got up to speed, but the streets here, even at this early hour were mostly empty. There was only one car between us. I closed the gap and followed her, wondering what I would do if she saw me. The light rail and markings on the park service truck are not in your face like Miami-Dade, but they're still visible.

Dropping back, I stayed far enough away that I hoped she could only see my headlights. I followed until she turned left on a gravel road. Pulling up to the turnoff, I waited for the red lights to recede and then followed. These roads were level and straight. As long as she couldn't see the light rail and I didn't appear to be threatening, I'd blend into the scenery. Five minutes later, I saw her brake lights flash and the car slowed before turning.

I followed, wary that she might have suspected a tail and almost pulled off on the road's shoulder. Instead, I decided to drive past and then turn around if it was warranted. Even if she were waiting, a park service truck going by at the speed limit shouldn't alarm her this close to the Everglades. She'd entered a short, narrow driveway and was exiting the Jeep. I sped past, quickly found a wide place in the road, made a fast U-turn, switched off my lights, and pulled off the road a couple hundred feet short of the entrance to the driveway.

A new set of headlights left the drive piercing the dark night and cutting through the mist that had started to set in. The lights belonged to a truck that pulled onto the road and turned away from me. It looked familiar and I didn't need to get closer to know who it was. The truck was identical to mine.

12

I was stuck between a rock and a hard place. The MACE twins were clearly up to something and after my visit to the bait shop and learning that a woman had bought the menhaden oil only days before Edward was murdered made them the prime, and only suspects. Checking my watch, I saw it was almost ten and I wondered what Susan was doing out here so late. I had seen her swoon at Amos. Maybe she had her own means of investigating a murder. Me, I'd stick to work.

Susan was likely heading home. If she was up to something else, it was none of my business. Tomorrow would be soon enough to confront her. While sitting in my car on the shoulder of the road, I looked at my phone and saw only one bar of service. After pecking out a quick text to Justine, I took a screenshot of my location, and headed back toward Miami. My plan was to swing by the crime lab and see if Justine could match the menhaden oil I had just bought to whatever skin samples had been taken off Edward's body.

Highway 41 is a dark and lonely road. Pairs of narrow-set eyes reflected back at me as I drove, and I suspected there were more alligators than people out here. Once in a while I saw headlights approach, and I gripped the wheel tighter as the oncoming vehicle passed me on the narrow road. Any wrong move would put me in the swamp.

I tried to piece together the crime as I drove. The motive appeared to be clear. MACE, and by extension Amos and Adrian wanted to shut down the power plant. The crocodiles and protest were smoke and mirrors. Edward's murder and the subsequent protest brought them a ton of free publicity. To those that put little value on human life, using Edward as a sacrifice was an easy to make it look like FP&L was behind the murder. But why Edward?

Just as I reached the Turnpike, the border of civilization, things changed quickly. As soon as I hit the main road traffic became heavy and as typical of this time of night, there were a handful of cars swerving, driving too fast, driving too slowly, or just not paying attention. It took all my concentration just to get to the crime lab in one piece. When I pulled up, I realized I was thinking about seeing Justine, and not the case.

The parking lot was nearly empty. I didn't see the van and she hadn't returned my texts. Not uncommon if she had been called into the field. I pulled into a space far enough from the door that the park service truck wouldn't be too noticeable. Technically we worked for different agencies, but you never knew how people looked at things, especially some of the headstrong detectives I had seen working for Miami-Dade. Just as I turned off the truck my phone vibrated and I breathed a sigh of relief when I read her message: *get down here*.

She wouldn't have to ask me twice. I had a feeling her urgency was more about the case than seeing me, but I'd take what I could get. My gut was right; when I walked in the door of her lab with the gallon of fish oil in my hand, she didn't notice me. I had to laugh at myself while I waited for her to realize I was standing there. I knew the fish oil would please her more than a dozen roses. Her long braid moved to the beat of the music that I could plainly hear through her headphones and I moved toward her, trying to catch her off-guard.

People have a sense when there is someone close by and just as I was about to kiss her neck she turned and almost hit me. I dodged the punch and settled for a quick "Hey". There was no kiss, but at least she acknowledged me by making enough room so I could slide in next to her monitor.

The screen on the left showed a picture of the tire tracks from the crime scene. The right screen showed what looked like a catalog of tread patterns.

"I found the tire. Now I need to cross-reference where it's sold."

It sounded like busy work to me, but she was clearly excited. "It's an off-brand, only available at a few stores and dealers."

That was interesting. My first thought was that she was trying to match the tire tread to the make and model of the vehicle. Rarely do people replace their car tires at the dealership, but UTVs were more of a specialty. "So, we can get their sales records and see if one of their customers matches anyone we know?" I played along.

"Something like that. I looked them up. They're called Gators. Made by John Deere."

I smiled at the irony of buying Gators in crocodile country. She pulled up the local dealer's website. The green and yellow off-road vehicles matched the FP&L fleet.

"It's one of theirs."

That hardly narrowed it down. I could only imagine how many Gators FP&L bought every year.

She read the look on my face. "Tread patterns are like fingerprints. You just have to take the picture and canvas the lot at Turkey Point. I'm betting you'll get a hit."

It sounded like thankless work. "If you print me out a copy, I'll run by in the morning and see if we can get a match." A brief image of Susan bending over to examine tire treads brought a smile to my face. Even if it didn't turn up anything it would be worth it.

"Hey, what's that?" She pointed at the jug on the desk.

"Just a little present for you," I said. "Careful, it's potent stuff."

"I bet, if you buy it in an unmarked plastic bottle," she reached for it.

She was like a little girl at Christmas. I was right when I guessed it was better than bringing roses. "Menhaden oil," I explained, wanting to warn her before she opened it.

"You sure know how to turn a girl on." Surprisingly, I think she was—turned on, that is.

"Aw, shucks. We just go out in the woods and spread this on and let the love happen."

"You and yourself," she said, after taking a whiff of the contents. "What is this?"

"Remember how the body had a smell to it, and the skin was kind of slimy? I have a theory that it was baited. Out in the airboat, Steve said that a crocodile would rarely attack something as large as a human." I explained to her how I had gone out to Redlands and wandered into the bait store.

"And I have skin samples," she said, jumping up from the stool. I grabbed the photo of the tire tread from the printer and followed her over to a stainless steel table. "Wait here. I have to check them out of the evidence locker."

I sat there staring at the picture of the tire tread and waited. We had two clues now, the tire treads and menhaden oil. I looked over at the jug and down at the picture and knew they weren't going to solve the case, but they might point us in the right direction. Though it would give me a little revenge for the gun incident to see Susan on her hands and knees inspecting tires in the parking lot, I suspected the vehicles were not assigned but rather used as needed. Without an empty bottle with fingerprints on it or security footage from the bait store, the menhaden oil was also a dead end. I had thought about running some pictures by the clerk, but that rarely worked.

The clues might give us direction, but I still needed motive. For a crime as serious as premeditated murder, unless you had a serial killer on the loose—sex, greed, and revenge were the short list. If Amos and/or Adrian had committed a crime of this magnitude without any of the usual motives it would be pure evil: Edward would have been a human sacrifice—or he knew something.

As the attorney for MACE, he would be privy to where the proverbial bodies were buried and with an organization like that there were bound to be skeletons. I wondered if I was spending too much time on the physical evidence and should instead be looking for the real motive. Shutting down the power plant was not enough reason. Tomorrow I would have Susan checking tire treads while I delved into the legal side of MACE. I wasn't sure how I was going to do this, but I had an idea that's where I would find some answers.

Justine came back in with a small cooler. She brought it to the table, opened it, and removed several glass jars. "Skin samples from our friend."

This was her element. While she started to lay everything out, my mind had slid to another dimension. If not for my girlfriend brushing up against me, I would be out of here. At least if Martinez chose to track my whereabouts, it would show the Miami-Dade crime lab, not some backwoods residence of one of the suspects.

Justine had several slides set out on the counter. On one she placed a few drops of the menhaden oil. Then with a pair of tweezers she carefully removed a small sample from the jar and placed it on another slide. After placing the images side-by-side, she looked at the screen and she shook her head. "I need to use our gas chromatograph. I can't get past the organic material to get a match."

"The smell test tells me they're the same."

"Tell that to a jury," she said, starting to clean up. She placed the sample back in the cooler. "My place?"

I smiled, then remembered Mariposa's invitation. "Remember Mariposa?"

"Sure, the nice lady that works at your office."

"Any interest in going to her house for dinner tomorrow night?"

"And you're asking me now?"

I thought for a second that she had seen through my procrastination. "She just asked earlier."

"That'd be fun."

"Awesome." I meant it. "See ya in a bit?"

"I'm two steps behind you. Just have to log this back in," she said, taking the cooler and following me out the door.

I breathed a sigh of relief both for finally satisfying Mariposa's invitation, but also for making a real date with Justine. Twenty minutes later, I used my key to let myself into her apartment, vowing this time, to stay awake until she got home.

13

My phone woke me again. I thought it might be morning and I had again failed in my mission to stay awake. Glancing at the screen, I saw it was a text from Justine, and only thirty minutes after I had arrived at her apartment. With my thumb, I unlocked the screen and read the message: *Got a dead one, call me.*

Her phone went to voicemail, telling me she was probably already at the crime scene and unable to answer. I knew this could take all night and thought about my options. Maybe the best was to take off and head home. That is not as easy as it sounds when you live on an island, but the wind was down and the skies were clear. Transiting the bay in my center console in the dark was not my idea of fun, though I was getting more comfortable with it.

I texted her back to call when she could and said that I was taking off to get an early start tomorrow. It had been several days since I had done my actual job and patrolled the park. If I knew it, Martinez certainly did too. He counted on the statistics created by wayward boaters and amateur drug dealers to keep his budget looking good and hold onto his job. With the ever-present cutbacks and this close to retirement, he was always at risk of being asked if he'd take the proverbial gold watch to free up some space. He needed the numbers to look good to justify his job. Park service pensions were good, but his golf habit was expensive.

Locking myself out, I went to the truck already second-guessing my decision to leave. Her calls didn't always take all night—there was still hope. Starting the truck, I knew it was too late to go back. I had already texted that I was leaving. Lesson learned: wait and think it out next time.

Traffic was surprisingly light this early in the morning. I rubbed my eyes, trying to clear the cobwebs from my head and remain alert. The few drivers out were either late remnants from the bar scene or very early-morning commuters probably working the Asian or European markets. Spotting patterns was something that came natural to me and I had noticed that the east coast ran on a later schedule than the west. Rush hour in the San Francisco Bay area and Southern California started as early as five am. The West Coast was always behind the curve with the financial markets, businesses, and government opening before the sun had even thought about rising over the Sierra Nevada Mountains.

I made it to Homestead, parked, and headed to my boat. The sight of the still water, reflecting the stars and illuminated by a sliver of moon resolved any apprehensions I had about crossing the bay at night. Some nights were ominous—tonight wasn't one of them. After untying the lines, I backed out of the slip, and started up the channel. Across the way, Bayfront Park was quiet, the fishermen and boaters were either out doing some night fishing on the reef or still asleep. As I entered the main channel I had to smile, even though I had missed a night with Justine. The only thing breaking the stillness was the sound of my outboard echoing across the mangroves.

I passed the last marker, pointed the bow of the boat toward Adams Key and accelerated. Just as the hull shot out of the still water and started to get up on plane, I felt the vibration of the phone in my pocket. Looking forward to the ride, I almost ignored it, thinking it was a funny thing that after only a few months here I had caught the boat bug. There is a feeling you get when the boat gets up on top of the water and starts skipping over the small waves at high speeds that's hard to describe and it's one that you want to keep going.

The only person who would be calling me this time of night was probably Justine and I'd rather get my jollies with her than the boat so I slowed down. The boat wallowed in its own wake and I pulled the phone from my pocket hoping to see her name on the screen. If it was someone else, I'd be mad.

My mindset shifted immediately when I read her text. Spinning the wheel, I turned the bow to face southwest and saw the reflection of the red, white, and blue lights of the emergency vehicles under the shadow of the twin chimneys guarding the Turkey Point plant. There had been another murder.

It wasn't hard to find the small dock since I had been there before, and less than five minutes later, I pulled up to it, and tied the boat off. Grabbing my gun belt and gear, I headed toward the flashing lights. Whatever had happened was out in the cooling canals and I had to hitch a ride from a close-mouthed security guard driving a UTV. Before I even reached the crime scene tape, I saw Rebecca Moore coming directly toward me.

"I'm so glad you're here," she said, taking my arm and leading me to the scene. Before crossing the line, she threw out a spoiler: "It's another one of those activists."

From her tone I was unsure if she was upset about the murder or how it would look for the plant. Holding the tape up for her with my free hand, I tried to pull away, but she clung onto me and steered me toward the action. Before I could extricate myself I saw Justine and Sid bent over the body of a woman—a tall woman. Some kind of female radar triggered Justine to look up as we approached and I couldn't help but see the expression on her face when she saw Rebecca's arm linked to mine. She turned back quickly.

A uniformed officer, whom I recognized from the other night as Grace Herrera's partner stopped us and asked for credentials. Rebecca could go no closer, but he nodded at me and reluctantly allowed me to pass. Up ahead Grace was talking to one of the plant's security guards. Now she looked at me and gave me a quick nod. Besides another dead body, I was stuck in a quagmire of estrogen.

"Hey," I said to the backs of Justine and Sid as I looked over their shoulders at the mangled face of the victim.

"Hey back," Justine said without turning back to me. "Got a friend of yours here."

"It's Adrian."

"Appears that way. Another activist attacked by a croc. Maybe these big guys are trying to tell us something."

Off in the distance I heard several groans coming from the water and wondered if the local population knew its days were probably numbered. Like the bears and wolves out west, when a gator, or in this instance a croc, attacked a person or livestock, they were hunted down and dealt with. There was often a lot of pressure not to put down the culprits and, in some situations, the animals were relocated. In this case, I suspected the worst. The Crocodile Lake National Wildlife Center was in North Key Largo, but I remembered Steve saying something about these crocodiles being sheltered in the canal system. They could flourish here, but likely not in the wild.

"I guess all your buddies are here," Justine said, without looking up.

I ignored the jab.

"Looks like the crocs got another one. Maybe that Miami-Dade officer that has her eyes on you will be next."

"I'm thinking they only like the taste of activists," I said, kneeling down and smelling the corpse. Sid shot a *"what the hell is he doing"* look to Justine who finally smiled. She couldn't stay mad very long with a dead body in front of her.

"We're working on a theory that the crocs are being baited," she explained to him and leaned over next to me. "Hope that date's still on for tomorrow night because smelling dead bodies isn't going to cut it for me."

"Okay, kids, whatever you've got going on between you, let's stow it and concentrate on what we've got here," Sid said.

The way Sid looked at each of us, with his bushy eyebrows raised, and waiting for us to acknowledge him reminded me of my grandfather. We did and he continued.

"Time of death looks to be about two hours ago. That would put it around 1am," he said, inspecting the long probe he had just removed from her liver. "No fishing for you tonight?" Sid asked, looking at me.

He laughed at his own joke and started packing his equipment. Justine moved in to take his spot and scraped a sample of Adrian's skin into a bag and tagged it. It was evidence, but I didn't need any tests to be run to know that it was the same menhaden oil used on Edward. I got up. "I'm going to have a look around and see if we can see where the body was hauled out. Looks like the attack was close." I could see the blood trail glistening in the work lights. There would be no footprint or claw-prints, as it were, in the hard gravel surface, but I could see blood and where the ground had been disturbed. It looked like a struggle had taken place and from the visible marks on Adrian, she had been conscious when the attack occurred.

"Slow down, Ranger Rick," Justine said. "I'll get to that as soon as Sid releases the body."

"Just looking around." Her fuse was either too short or I was in trouble again—maybe both. To make matters worse I saw Grace Herrera coming toward us.

"Agent Hunter," she said. "Sid, Justine."

They looked up and acknowledged her, but I could tell from the look on Justine's face that Grace was ruining her party.

"Can you release an ID or cause of death yet?" she asked Sid.

Sid looked at me, and then past me. I turned to follow his gaze and saw Rebecca coming at us. I had no idea how she had gotten inside the crime scene and from the determined look on her face, there was absolutely zero chance of this ending well.

"Folks, I'm wondering if the park service shouldn't take this case. There are clearly some similarities to the previous one," Rebecca said.

Before anyone else could speak, Grace made a move toward her. It wasn't aggressive, just a lioness claiming her turf. "Ma'am, the land here falls within Miami-Dade jurisdiction. The last body was found in the bay, within the parks boundaries. It looks to me like both agencies will be involved." She stepped closer to me.

"I know better than to speak for my boss," I said, hoping she would get the message. Susan for a partner was enough for me.

"Either way it goes, we were called and I'll have to file a report. Anything you can give me, Sid?"

He stood up. Even with his slight stoop from examining too many bodies over too many years, he was tall. "Okay, children. Let's play nicely. No information is being released until I complete the autopsy. The boy should be in by the time we get the body back. I'll let him help and we can work this up together and by lunchtime you should have your answers."

He laughed again. His relationship with Vance was odd. It took a special man to mentor his boss. His skillset apparently covered inter-agency squabbles as well. "Works for me," I said. I had already been awake for close to twenty-four hours and had gotten little sleep the two nights before. I turned to the FP&L attorney, knowing she was trying to use me. "I'll be in touch in the morning." Rebecca pouted but seemed happy with this. She knew that she had already pushed her limits and that she and I were not going to be getting together tonight. She thanked us all for doing such a professional job and walked away.

Grace was next, saying she'd be in touch after she spoke to her supervisor. That left only Justine, Sid and me, standing silently in a circle around the body.

Sid broke the spell. "Body's good to go." He walked toward the Medical Examiner's van, and asked the two deputies nearby to load the corpse.

Justine and I stared at the ground, then started to speak at the same time. It was a surreal moment in a sea of chaos. All around us different colored lights were flashing, people were talking and we had to move out of the way when the deputies approached with the gurney. We spoke with our eyes, each telling the other we were sorry.

It was understood and special, broken only by a wink of her eye before she followed the body toward the van.

That's my girl, I thought. *Taking a dead body over me.*

14

A SHOWER, change of clothes, and a few hours of sleep had me feeling better. That was, until I had to stand in front of Martinez. He was unusually subdued this morning and I was trying to figure out his mood while waiting for him to speak. I settled on it being Saturday, he had probably had to forgo his tee time. Finally, I had a case where I wasn't the one to find the body and the crime didn't take place within the park boundaries. He should be happy.

"If it weren't for the damned budget, I'd cut you loose on this case too, Hunter." He shook his head as if it were a sad thing. Maybe it was. If we could solve the case, there'd be a lot of positive media coverage for us.

I had my own problems. It was bad enough having to work with Susan as a pseudo partner. Adding Grace to the mix was a cocktail I had no taste for. Still, maybe it was stubbornness, but I wanted the case.

Seeing him this way gave me an in and I pried the knife into the oyster. "The cases are clearly related." I started to lay out my argument. "Let Miami-Dade run with it. I know the detective that's handling the case. Maybe we can set up some kind of liaison arrangement with them." He looked up from his papers.

"That could work. Let them use their resources and you just tag along for the ride. I like that."

I knew he would. Now I added the closer. "Susan might be a problem though. She doesn't get along with detective Herrera all that well. Could be some friction."

At first, I thought I had gone too far, but the odds of finding another reason to lose Susan as my partner might never come along. I was still upset about spotting her at Amos's last night and I expected sooner, rather than later, he would consult his overnight surveillance feeds and discover we were both at the house where the latest victim had been, just hours before the attack.

"I'll handle her," he said. "Just try to wrap this up quickly. We've got a couple of big weeks coming up out there."

He was referring to the two weeks around the holidays. If the weather held, the week between Christmas and New Year was one of our busiest seasons. *Busy* here meant tourists that would pad his stats before the year ended. "I'll check on the autopsy and see how Miami-Dade is doing with the investigation this morning."

"Remember, Hunter, the key word here is to let *them* do the work. If I were you, I'd get a couple of hours of patrol in and let them handle the heavy lifting."

That didn't surprise me and I was fine with it. There were more layers to this case than what I was wearing to fight off the morning chill. With a brisk wind blowing cold air from the north, I didn't expect much boating action out there. Throwing a few flies might give me a new perspective.

"Okay," I said, and got up to leave. "I'll be out till about noon, then I can check in with the medical examiner and Miami-Dade."

"Remember your report," he called to me as I was leaving.

Of course, the paperwork that kept the bureaucracy going was more important than the results. While hoping to get out of the building before Susan came in I looked at Mariposa's empty desk, remembering our date for tonight. My window for getting anything done today was quickly shrinking.

Saturdays are usually busy. Today was different with the cold front that had dipped into the region last night, leaving a biting north wind and dropping the temperature into the fifties this morning. I expected by noon the subtropical sun, if it broke through, would add about twenty degrees, but seventy is still on the cool side here.

Leaving the building I pulled a sweatshirt on over my park service shirt to fight the cold. Having lived in the mountains out west, I was used to much colder temperatures, but as they say it's a dry cold. Fifty degrees here felt like every bit of twenty. After releasing the lines, I pulled the boat out of the slip, and just as I turned the bow toward the channel, looked back at headquarters. Susan was just pulling in and I wondered how that was going to go. Would Martinez actually pull her from the case, or would he pacify her with some kind of concession?

I had to pull back on the throttle after I saw how my subconscious had pushed the speed past the no-wake limit in an attempt to get away from these people. Without thinking, my hands turned the wheel to starboard and I headed toward the smokestacks of the Turkey Point plant.

There were several boats fishing near the outflow from the plant's gas-fired generator. On a cold morning like this the fish sought the warmer water. Ahead, Chico stood like a statue on his poling platform, scanning the water for the telltale sign of a head or tail breaking the surface. The chop would make it all but impossible to sight fish this morning, but the guides didn't have a choice.

I tried to give him some space, but just as I passed, he eased down onto the deck and started the engine. For a second, I thought he was coming after me and I slowed until I saw the bend in the angler's rod. He was hooked up to something big, probably a tarpon. Chico ran forward and released the anchor, leaving it to drift on a large red buoy. When the fight was over he would recover it. Now, free to pursue the fish, he encouraged his client to pull it away from the mangroves.

It was like slow motion when the silver king jumped. Trying to shake the hook, water flew from its scales, and the fish landed with a splash. I looked over at the angler who, with Chico behind him—

coaching every step, was slowly making progress. Most of the tarpon, especially this time of year, are juveniles. Even so, it probably weighed thirty pounds. The fish, often topping a hundred pounds, move around constantly looking for the perfect water temperature which gives them both comfort and food. Today, the power plant was it.

They had the fish close to the boat when I heard an outboard closing in. It was moving fast, and I reached into the glove compartment for my gun belt. There was no posted speed limit here, but from the sound of the motor, it was coming straight toward us, and at a dangerous speed. It wouldn't be an angler. There was fierce competition, especially among the guides, but there were also common courtesies. The wake and noise from the approaching craft would scare the fish, or at least shut down the bite.

I chanced a look at the offending vessel and was shocked to see the green park service fabric on the T-top. It was Susan and she was coming right for me. Whatever Martinez had said, or more likely didn't say, was going to result in a showdown.

Chico also looked at her. This could cost him the fish. With the weather the way it was, it might be his only bite today. I silently prayed that he landed it. The guides talked, and after my poorly phrased question yesterday, and Susan roaring through the fishing grounds this morning, all the work I had tried to do to cultivate a friendship would be wasted. Patrolling an area this size, you needed other eyes and ears. These guys were on the water almost every day and knowledgeable about what went on here. Losing them as a source for information would be devastating to the park.

"Slow down," I yelled, then picked up the VHF microphone and tried to hail her. There was no change in speed and no answer on the radio, not that I expected any. She was within a hundred yards now and still running wide open.

Chico was trying to push the angler, knowing what was coming would make it harder to land the fish. He was bent over, working the leader toward the boat when the first wake hit, rocking the shallow draft boat and forcing him to the deck. I could see the scowl on his face when the leader went tight and the fish ran. He gained his feet and looked over at us.

While I had been watching Chico, Susan had maneuvered her boat next to mine. She sat several feet off my port side. The wake caught up to us and I had to grab the posts holding the T-top for support. "What the hell?" I called over to her. "These guys are trying to fish."

"Screw that. There was another murder last night and you didn't call me?"

I wondered whether she had talked to Martinez yet or just jumped on her boat to come after me. It wouldn't have been the first time. "It was late and I was here already." I didn't want to let on that I knew where she had been. "It was Adrian. Looks like she was killed the same way as Edward." I hoped that giving her information she either already had or could easily get might defuse her.

"Amos has an alibi," she said, almost too quickly.

I looked at the other boats to see if they were listening. Fortunately, the tide was running out and we were drifting away from them. Chico was back on his knees, this time with the fish by the boat. I watched while he released the fish and slapped a high-five with the angler. Silently saying a quick thank you to whomever was listening, I turned back to her. "Can we take this somewhere else?"

"Back to the office," she said. Turning away, she pushed the throttle to the limit and spun the wheel toward Bayfront Park. I hoped the charter captains were all watching as the bow of her boat smashed into the choppy wind-driven waves and sent spray flying all over the deck. Just as the water hit her she throttled back and the boat immediately slowed before the next wave hit.

"Damned woman deserved that one," Chico said, idling off my starboard side. "This is my boy, Ralph. He's just back from school for the winter break. Charter cancelled on me—too cold."

"Winter break" sounded strange sitting here in Biscayne Bay, but a gust hit, reminding me how cold it was and I thought about how miserable Susan must be after taking that wave. "Awesome. Hey, sorry about yesterday."

"It's nothing. You just never know if your clients are purists, and doping flies is bad business for some."

"Got it. I think that guy was right about the menhaden oil."

"Good. Should have guessed those guys from Michigan would be cool."

"I'll talk to Susan about respecting your space out here."

"That one's been around for a while. We've seen this show before. Don't worry, we know it's not all of you."

Just most of us, I thought. Landing the tarpon had put him in a good mood. "You're out here all the time," I said. What's the deal with the crocs and environmental groups?"

I didn't expect what came next.

"We'd all be happy in the long run if this plant went to cooling towers and abandoned the canals. Salinity is a big issue in the bay, as is heat transfer. Even though the canals are not directly connected to the bay water, the aquifer is shallow enough that there has to be seepage. There's some rumor about radioactivity in the water here too. No one's been able to prove it, but I'm betting pretty soon these fish are going to have three eyes."

"And those two-faced environmentalists. They'll use the crocodiles, who never thrived here until the canals were cut in the seventies, to try and make this whole damned area a preservation zone. They want it all."

I think I had the last corner of that puzzle now. By making it appear that the crocodiles were aggressive, they would be looked on differently and the nanny lawmakers would shut down the whole area. The question was who would benefit from that outcome?

"Interesting how many layers this has," I said louder than I intended. I thanked Chico and headed back toward Adams Key. I needed to follow through on the autopsy, check in with Grace, and use my private office. The last thing I needed was Susan hovering over me at headquarters.

15

HALF AN HOUR LATER, I arrived at Adams Key. I heard Zero barking and braced myself for his standard greeting, but he was behind the closed door of Becky and Ray's house. Their boat was gone, and I figured they were on their weekly shopping trip. After securing the lines, I went up the path to my house.

I made a pot of coffee and checked the time. It was almost noon and I texted Justine to see if we were still on for tonight. While I waited for her to respond, I took a cup to the high counter and started punching in some of the keywords I had gotten from Chico into Google.

What I found was a convoluted mess. If you wanted to find a motive for anything from bribery to murder, it was there. There was no wonder that Rebecca had a full-time job working for FP&L. They were constantly under siege, both from environmental groups, the local jurisdictions, and the feds. Claims ranging from the increased salinity and noticeable levels of radiation in the bay to polluted drinking water were being brought against them.

It wasn't a simple matter to dissect the web of lawsuits and agreements. It appeared that FP&L was the defendant in all of them and I began to wonder how the plant was still in operation. Built in the

1970s, it was clearly out of date—the canals were leaking but still in use. An experimental method of cooling the super-heated wastewater by pumping it deep into the ground was being tested. So far, the reviews I'd read were mixed. I already knew that South Florida sat on a bed of porous coral and limestone, and wondered how they thought that by injecting the water deep into the earth it would not affect the drinking water.

They were essentially given ten years to fix everything, which is a very long time in environmental years. Cooling towers were the apparent answer, but then the animal activists came into play trying to protect the crocodiles.

Making the crocodiles look like murderous thugs would clearly put this last group on the defensive. I still had in my mind the image of Amos and Adrian smiling at each other after the rally. Other than that there was no indication, aside from their sharing an office, that they got along. Her visit to his house the other night could have just as easily been hostile as friendly. I had seen Susan pull out just as Adrian had pulled in. That couldn't be a coincidence.

That left MACE, still as the primary suspect—but now with Adrian dead, that no longer made sense.

I stared at the screen searching for answers and was well into my second cup of coffee when my phone vibrated. It was Justine. She said she'd just been out for a paddle and would be there for dinner with Mariposa and her husband. She would meet me at the headquarters building later.

With that off my mind, I tried to focus on what was in front of me. My head was spinning and I decided some exercise was in order. I put my phone in its waterproof case to let Martinez think I was still working and changed into board shorts and a T-shirt. After dragging the kayak to the dock, I grabbed a spinning rod and paddle from the side of the house. A few minutes later, I had crossed Caesar Creek and entered the maze of mangrove islands, channels, and lagoons known as Islandia.

Mullet jumped under the mangroves and I cast a silver spoon in their direction. Nothing took it and I decided to troll around.

Avoiding the area where I had found Abbey Bentley's body a few weeks ago, I paddled deeper into the mangroves. The cold front had either stalled or passed and the air was quickly warming back to its usual winter temperature of seventy degrees. The wind had dropped as well. Still, nothing hit the spoon and I decided to try my luck on the ocean side.

Staying close to the shoreline, I paddled out of the channel and into open water. Several wakes passed under me, rocking the kayak from side to side, as boaters headed out to take advantage of the better weather. There was still no action and I blamed it on the cold front, and remembered the guides all fishing outside the power plant this morning.

I recalled from my tour with Bob, and some later Google Earth reconnaissance, that Turkey Point was actually two separate plants. The nuclear and traditional gas-fired facilities were as interwoven as the bay's eco-systems. The nuclear facility needed the cooling canals and the fossil fuel generator used the outflow into the bay. From the satellite images, it was hard to tell where one ended and the other began.

Both the fishermen and the crocodiles benefited from the warm water. Chico held a long-term view of things and I wondered if the other guides did as well. The answer had to lie somewhere within that close-mouthed group, MACE, or in the network of waterways. Bob had shown me what he or his superiors wanted me to see. I wanted to look on my own. Sitting close to the mangroves in the kayak—I realized I had the right vehicle for the job.

I paddled hard back to Adams Key and hauled the kayak into the center-console. There was not enough time to paddle to Turkey Point and back—even if I wanted to. It was also about a fifteen-mile round trip across open water.

Bringing a change of clothes for later in a dry bag, I hopped down to the center-console, released the lines, and headed across the bay. Martinez might wonder at the zigzag lines on his screen when he checked it on Monday and I'd have to get a little creative in my report.

Rationalizing that the kayak was for exploratory purposes only, I used the center-console to get within a few hundred yards of the outflow canal. With the boat anchored out of sight, behind a large mangrove point, I loaded up on disposable gloves and evidence bags, put my phone with them in the waterproof bag, and slid the kayak into the water. Boarding the small craft from another boat was a lot harder than it looked and I patted myself on the back for bringing a change of clothes after I flipped over on my first try.

Thankful the water was shallow and the air was twenty degrees warmer than this morning. I paddled hard over to the canals and beached the kayak. Slipping on the flip-flops I had stashed behind the seat, I took the dry bag with the evidence gear and headed up the embankment that led to the first canal.

The wildlife the system was purported to support was evident the minute I reached the top of the bank. It was a ten-square-mile mini-ecosystem. Egrets, herons, and pelicans were scattered around the miles of shoreline and the black ducks that frequent saltwater cruised the surface dipping their heads every so often to scoop up a baitfish. Larger predators were also evident, breaking the water as they competed for the same food as the birds. Though most of the residents of the canals were common in South Florida, they looked to be undisturbed here. I observed this just as I saw the *No Trespassing* signs installed every twenty feet along the top of the berm.

Staying low, I followed the loose gravel road to the area where I had found the tire tracks after the first murder. With an eye toward the access road where Bob had entered with the UTV, I started walking along the path from where I remembered the long washed away tire tracks had ended and the water began.

I reached what I thought was the right area. The ground here was much softer and I almost fell descending the berm. When I got to within a few feet of the water I started to sink. I took off my flip-flops and continued down the slope barefoot. At the water's edge, I thought I saw the snout of a waiting croc, and turned to start back up, when I saw what looked like a boot print. The front of the impression was intact. The heel was missing and I assumed whoever had left it had climbed out by digging their toes in like you would in a snow bank.

The depth, angle, and open back of the footprint must have let the rain run out of it, allowing the impression to survive the storm.

Standing there with my feet stuck in the mud, I took my phone out of the waterproof case and took several pictures of the print from every height and angle I could without moving. Next, I took out an evidence bag and brushed some of the nearby dirt and gravel into it. Something was familiar about it, but my mind drew a blank and I continued with my search.

My next move proved to be harder than I expected. Calf-deep in the mud, I tried to pull my legs free, but the suction held them. Dropping to all fours, I used my hands to crawl up the bank and finally my feet slid out of the muck. By the time I reached the top, I was covered in mud.

There was no way I was going back into the canal to wash it off, and as the hot sun began to cake it onto my skin, I started back to the kayak satisfied that I had accomplished something. I was almost there when I heard the roar of an off-road vehicle. Wondering if my presence had attracted attention I tried to locate the source. With my hand on my brow to shield the sun that was now low in the sky I saw what I thought were two men in a UTV.

It looked like they had just passed the access point to the canal system. To reach me they would have to make their way around dozens of turns. It was impossible to tell from the direction they were heading if they were coming for me or not.

They started down the perimeter road and I watched the driver accelerate through the turn. I wondered what the urgency was as I watched the UTV bounce and slide along the road. The driver sped up into the second turn much like a race driver and skidded along the bank and almost landed in the adjacent canal. The tires caught and he followed the next canal to the turn. To my surprise they stopped there.

Curious, I moved closer. It was hard to judge distance, but I was able to count four canals between us and figured they were about a quarter mile away. Looking down at myself, I thought the mud camouflage could have made me invisible, and when I heard the crack of a rifle. I dropped to the ground thinking they were shooting first and asking questions later.

Checking myself, I found no wounds and crawled to my knees. Another shot rang out and I saw one of the men go after something on the bank of the canal across from where they had parked. He stopped, reached down, and came up with what looked like a long winding tube. It must have been one of the Burmese Pythons Steve said had invaded this part of the county. Walking back to the UTV, he tossed it into the pickup bed. The two men high-fived and grabbed what looked like fishing poles from the back.

A few minutes later, I had crept to within two canals and could clearly see the men sitting on the bank drinking beers and tossing lures at the captive fish. One of the rods bent and the man hauled a nice-sized peacock bass out of the canal. Getting to his feet, he slung it into the pickup bed of the Gator. It wasn't me they had seen. I had just stumbled onto their private game preserve.

Creeping even closer, I pulled the phone from its case and snapped several pictures before turning to move back down the embankment that abutted the bay. Immediately I sank to my knees again, but I preferred that to being seen—or worse.

Or at least that's what I thought until I tried to extricate myself from the muck. I got one leg out and looked over at the two men who apparently hadn't noticed my struggle. The other leg was stuck deeper. I pulled hard, having the advantage of three limbs this time and it started to move, then came free with a loud sucking sound. The silence was broken, and a flock of birds took off behind me. I think it was that and not me that attracted the men's attention, but it didn't matter. Before I could gain my feet, the sound of their shotgun echoed across the canals. I saw the pellets break the surface of the water just behind me and thought I was clear until I heard the more distinct sound of a rifle and a bullet embedded itself in the dirt by my feet.

Staying in a crouch, I ran and slid toward the bank. Instinctively, I swerved in my course, moving away from where the previous bullet had landed and not allowing the shooter to adjust his aim.

I finally reached the kayak. Just as I dipped the blade into the water, I heard the roar of the UTV coming toward me. I paddled hard and by the time they reached the bank, I was around the corner and stopped to catch my breath, wondering how far these men would go to protect their canals.

16

I HAULED the kayak aboard and started the center-console. Staying tight against the mangroves, I hugged the shore on the way back to Bayfront Park. It took a little longer, but I appreciated the cover of the dense brush. Coated in mud as I was, I doubted the men knew who they were shooting at. Since the park service boat was hidden behind the point I was sure that I had not been identified.

In my rush to get back, I cut the corner of the channel a little too tight and was grateful there was no one to see the stream of silt being kicked up by the propeller. I slowed and took a deep breath. If my goal was to stay incognito, I wasn't accomplishing it covered in mud and running the flats in the park service boat.

Taking my time now, I was soon in the turning basin and docked the boat. Looking down at myself, I decided a quick swim might help as a pre-wash to remove enough of the mud and muck to look less like the creature from the black lagoon if anyone saw me. I knew I would still need a long shower before our date. Climbing onto the park service dock, I saw Justine coming toward me.

I paused to admire her and also get a sense of whether she was mad or not before hauling myself out of the water. She looked stunning. The color of her sundress accented her deeply tanned legs and highlighted her eyes. She strode toward me with a smile on her face.

"This some new kind of date prep?" she asked, keeping her distance as I hauled myself out of the water.

"You like it?"

She looked at her watch. "Maybe you could have started this ritual a little sooner. We're going to be late."

"Give me ten minutes and I'll be ready. I've got a story that's worth it."

"I bet you do."

Several minutes later with the hot water streaming over me, I scrubbed the mud from my body. It took several wash, rinse, and repeats to get it all off and I wondered what the allure of mud baths was supposed to be. I toweled off and started to dress, aware that I was totally outclassed by Justine. I had only a Hawaiian shirt and shorts. Thankfully they were flat-fronts and not the cargo shorts I usually wore. Without another change of clothes, I was stuck. Although we'd been dating for several months, we'd never really gone out anywhere. Forget the "really", I thought, realizing how lame a boyfriend I must be as I walked down the stairs to the lobby. When she got up I froze. On the dock I had only gotten a quick glance, but seeing her here, with the sundress highlighting all the right parts and her hair braided tightly in a single French braid that accented her face she took my breath away. I could detect only the lightest touch of makeup, maybe some mascara, but that was all. Perfect couldn't have looked better.

"You look like you've seen a ghost."

"Hardly. You look spectacular."

A trace of red rose in her face. "Not too bad yourself. Those your dress flip-flops?"

I hadn't brought a change in footwear and had to take my flip-flops into the shower with me to try and clean them. Looking down at my feet, I saw I had missed a few spots. "You have me at a disadvantage."

"Let's keep it that way. Ready?"

"Yup. Let's roll." I led her out of the building, activated the alarm, and locked the door behind me. Things had gotten a lot more convenient since Martinez had given me keys. For a second, I had a panic attack that they might be GPS enabled like everything else that was issued, but then I realized there was a simpler way. The alarm system would have a record of who entered, exited, and when.

At least I had something to show for my afternoon's exploration and I told Justine the story in between interruptions from Siri giving us directions. About twenty minutes later we reached the address Mariposa had given me. It was a well-kept house in a newer post-Andrew neighborhood. I had learned pretty quickly that the hurricane was how people kept time here. Justine grabbed a bag from around her feet and followed me to the door.

She had a bottle of wine with her and I felt myself drop more than a few rungs on the good-boyfriend ladder. If we were going to stay at level five, I'd better up my game. "Thanks for that," was all I could say before I pressed the button for the doorbell.

"*De nada,*" she answered.

Maybe this was how a good relationship worked, with one partner naturally covering for the other. She might not think anything of it, but I did, and vowed to be more attentive to such details in the future.

The wine was well received and the rum was spectacular. There were no soft drinks to mix it with—this was straight sipping rum. Raul, Mariposa's husband was in his element, giving a lesson on how to appreciate the Appleton 21-year-old. Bronze-colored and smokey, with a hint of vanilla, the rum was indeed special. Mainly a beer drinker, I instantly acquired a taste until Justine sneaked her phone over, and showed me that the stuff cost over a hundred dollars a bottle. As good as it was, and over protests from our host, I turned down a refill.

Dinner was equally spectacular with a coconut-curried chicken. Mariposa said she had learned the recipe with goat, and I silently thanked her for the change. Fried plantains and an ice cream I had never heard of capped off the night. Justine seemed to be enjoying herself and laughed freely, but looking over at her, all I wanted to do was take her home.

The mood was broken when my phone vibrated. It was a text from Susan and I knew the day's reprieve from her had been too good to be true.

SOS.

That's all it said. I had to excuse myself to process this. Fortunately, Mariposa and Justine had started clearing the dessert dishes and Raul had snuck another taste of rum.

I found the bathroom, closed the door, and leaned against the counter. Susan would not have texted me if she were not in trouble. I pressed her contact info and then the locate-my-phone icon. It took longer than usual and I thought, after seeing where the blue dot was, that the great Google might have had trouble locating the spot in the middle of a dense green area with no apparent roads. I pressed the button for the map app and waited.

I decided against returning her text in case the call would endanger her further and zoomed into the vast swath of green—the Everglades. There weren't too many ways in or out of the river of grass and I was unfamiliar with most of them. The list of directions said I needed to find SW 168th Street, but even zooming in as much as the phone allowed didn't show a street by the flashing dot. But the area looked familiar and I suspected I knew where she was.

I had serious second thoughts about what I was going to do. With Raul happily enjoying what was probably his last glass of the premier rum for a while and dinner over, I didn't think it would be rude to leave, especially if I continued to drool over Justine. Mariposa had already noticed my infatuation and made several jokes at my expense.

Justine was the problem. I knew I shouldn't take her with me, but I didn't want this night to end. I was able to rationalize my decision on the basis that she had already saved my life once. I also didn't know what Susan was up to and, knowing her, this could as easily be a trap as a legitimate call for help. She could have just as easily texted

911 as SOS. Maybe having Justine as a witness wasn't a bad idea either.

I must have been too abrupt saying goodbye and I paid for it when we were out the door.

"What the hell was that about?" she asked, standing on the sidewalk with her hands on her hips.

Even mad, she looked beautiful, but I had to put that from my mind. I pulled my phone out and handed it to her with the text from Susan on the screen.

"What's with that woman?"

"Hell if I know." I allowed the frustration to seep into my voice. "I can't ignore it. Want to take a ride?"

She was still angry, but I caught a hint of excitement in her voice. "Sure, lure a girl into the Everglades and take advantage of her." She walked around to the passenger door and got in.

I let out a breath before getting into the driver's side. Before I switched back into special agent mode, I reached over and grabbed her. Taking her in my arms, I kissed her hard until reality finally tugged me away. "That's my plan. Take advantage of you until you throw me out," I said, with my face only inches from hers.

This time she pulled me in.

When we finally separated, there was a deep quiet in the truck as we caught our breath—it was time to go to work. "Ready?"

"Roger that," she said, smoothing out her dress.

Traffic was lighter now and I pushed the speed limit working my way west to the Turnpike. I thought about using the light bar on top of the truck, but the streamlined blue and white lights were almost embarrassing. I'd probably have a better chance of being pulled over for using the wannabe lights than speeding. After exiting the turnpike in Kendall I continued making my way south and west. The area looked familiar and when I saw a street sign I had a quick flashback to where Justine and I had taken down a crooked cop named Dwayne. I started to regret my decision to bring her, but it was too late.

Fortunately, the turn was before the city limits and we were spared reliving that night. Heading west, we passed agricultural fields that eventually turned into the sawgrass that ran for miles to the tip of the peninsula. The road narrowed to one and a half lanes and I had to dodge several gators and pythons in the road as I sped toward the dot. I was getting close when I saw the dull halo of light in the humid air and found the unmarked driveway. This was as far as I had been the other night when I had followed Adrian.

I thought about going in on foot, but the dangers of the Everglades and our sketchy footwear persuaded me to enter by the driveway. I turned in, cutting my headlights as I approached the large house. A newer four-wheel drive pickup was parked in front of a landscaped entrance. Susan's truck was off to the side of the driveway. Just before the dense vegetation ended I stopped, wondering what to do now. Moving any closer we would surely be seen.

I picked up my phone and started typing out a message to Susan that I was outside. Having no idea what the circumstances were of her SOS call, I was reluctant to barge into the house. I did pull out my gun and checked the chamber to make sure a round was loaded and ready if needed. Unfortunately, it was the only weapon I had.

Before I could hit *Send*, a scream broke the silence. I told Justine to stay put and with the gun in my right hand, I opened the door with my left. I knew I should call for backup, and turned to Justine to ask her, but before I could stop her, she was by my side. Another scream broke the silence. The call could wait. It would take them too long to get here.

17

With Justine behind me, we moved to the wooded perimeter, and using the brush for cover, slid to the corner of the two-story stucco-clad house. It was dark, but from what I could tell the two-story structure looked like it belonged on the water or a golf course; not out here in the middle of the Everglades. Light emanated from two large windows on the front of the house and with Justine behind me, I made my way toward them. I was careful of the dark rooms, knowing that we were actually more visible if someone was watching with the lights out than with the room fully illuminated. I looked around, checking for surveillance cameras.

Seconds later, the security system kicked in and two large dogs came bounding toward us. In the dim light, I could see they were Great Danes and relaxed slightly. With tails wagging as they barked, I guessed this was more a game to them than the seek and destroy mission I would have expected from a more aggressive breed.

"I got this," Justine whispered, lowering herself to their eye level, which was more of a stoop than a squat. She extended her free hand allowing them to sniff it. The barking quickly stopped and after a few calming words and scratches to the right places, they lost interest and moved away to the next squirrel.

We stayed in place for a few minutes to make sure the dogs had not set the owner on alert, but nothing perceivable changed inside the house. I guessed there were a lot of critters out here and the dogs' barking was a regular occurrence. There also weren't any neighbors to worry about. Resuming our approach, I peered into the closest window, which revealed a kitchen appointed with rich wood cabinets and stainless steel appliances. A massive island ended my view.

Another scream brought me to the next window revealing the other side of the great room. The room was massive with fireplaces on each end. A dining room table was in front, closest to me, and a living area was toward the back of the house. It was there that I saw two figures. Susan and Amos were clearly illuminated by the recessed lighting.

She was bound in a chair. He sat on a leather couch a few feet away with an oriental rug between them. I wasn't sure what to expect after receiving Susan's call, but this was not it. He sat with his head in his hands, looking up every so often at her and then toward the window like he was expecting someone. There was no aggression or remorse evident on his face or in his body language. He leaned forward and started talking to her. I wondered why, if he had gone through the effort to subdue and restrain her, he hadn't also gagged her. Knowing Susan as I did, it would have been the first thing I would do. Red-faced, she spat something back at him. He started talking again and it looked like he was pleading with her. I took my eyes off them for a minute and scanned the room. There were no weapons visible.

Justine was still by my side, as we walked to the front door. With my weapon drawn, I stood in a firing stance and motioned for Justine to ring the doorbell. She pressed the illuminated button and we waited. There was no chime and I was about to press it again when the door opened. I hadn't realized how tall Amos was until I saw him in the eight-foot doorway. He had to be close to seven feet tall.

"Come in, Detective," he said, and looked over at Justine, "Ma'am."

He said it invitingly, like he was glad I was there. I distrusted the tone and moved past him, holding my weapon extended with both hands and sweeping the room for an invisible threat.

"If I meant you harm, you'd be dead. I heard the dogs and saw you on the camera. I think this is not the way you perceive it."

I wasn't sure what to say. Motioning him to stay put with the barrel of the gun, I walked sideways toward the living room and Susan. Amos remained in place with his arms folded across his chest like he was patiently waiting for me to figure out that he was innocent. Justine had already determined his innocence and was standing next to him. Still watching him, I moved to Susan and stared at her pleading face.

"Keep an eye on her, Detective," Amos said from the foyer. "She's had a little too much to drink."

I looked around the room once more before pulling out my knife to cut the duct tape restraining her, but then paused. I wanted to get a better idea of the situation before I released her. I wasn't exactly toying with her on purpose, but she perceived it that way and started groaning behind the gag. I looked over at Amos and he shrugged. He must have taped her mouth before he came to answer the door. There was nothing I could say. I would have silenced her too.

There was a quarter full bottle of what appeared to be an expensive whiskey I had never heard of on a low table by the couch. The etched glass bottle probably cost more than the brand I drank. Sitting next to the whiskey was a tray containing two glasses and an ice bucket full of large, square ice cubes.

I've had to deal with my fair share of drunks, bears, and meth heads and I'd say that bears are more predictable and the meth heads are the most dangerous, especially in withdrawal. As far as the drunks go, there's nothing scarier than an inebriated woman, not to be chauvinistic about it. I'd never say it out loud—that's just my observation.

Questions flashed through my mind about what was going on here. Susan glared at me and I figured the only way to find out was to unleash the beast. With a single cut the duct tape holding her hands together parted. She immediately reached for the tape over her mouth and pulled it off.

"Arrest him," she screamed at me.

I was on uneven ground here and unsure what to do. Susan appeared to be more of a threat than Amos. He was clearly not a man to be underestimated if he had subdued and secured an obviously drunk Susan McLeash. I looked for her sidearm, then realized she was still on probation and unarmed.

"Arrest him and get me out of here!" she ordered.

"How about you take a seat over there," I called to Amos, pointing the barrel of my pistol to the far end of the couch. "Maybe we can sort this out."

"There is nothing to sort out, you idiot," Susan screamed.

I looked at Justine who stood off to the side studying Amos and Susan. I wondered about her take on this scene. Before I could ask, I heard a strange sound behind me. It turned out to be more unexpected than strange. It was Susan, rocking back and forth sobbing; classic volatile drunk behavior. I ignored it, already dreading the unavoidable drive home with her.

Amos walked easily to the couch as if he didn't have a care in the world and sat where I indicated. "I'd offer you a drink, but under the circumstances that might not be a good idea," he said, crossing his long legs.

I was thankful I had stopped at one earlier. "You want to tell me what's going on here?" I asked Susan.

"Charge him with sexual assault. He tried to get me drunk and take advantage of me," she said in a half sob, half bark.

I'd seen this show before. I mostly dealt with poachers and drug dealers, but I had seen my share of domestic disputes. I looked over at Amos.

"Nice woman, but can't handle her liquor. I was about to make us some dinner when she attacked me from behind."

"You wanted it and you know it," she screamed now.

The fire was back in her eyes and I knew I had to tread lightly. "So, you're the victim here?"

"I would never file a complaint against a woman, especially an officer of the law."

For some reason I believed him. Susan looked like she was about to eat him for dinner. "Why don't we get out of here." I turned away from her and studied the room to make sure I hadn't missed anything.

She cast her eyes at the floor. "That's it? You're going to let him go?"

I looked at her again, trying to appear compassionate, even though I was ready to kill her myself. Instead I motioned to the door. "Let's go. We can sort this out in the morning when everyone has a clear head."

"I'll get you for this," she spat at Amos.

He sat with his legs crossed and his hands in his lap. You didn't get where he had by being over-reactive, but his calmness was almost as unsettling as her acting out. "I'll get in touch with you tomorrow morning," I said to him and escorted Susan out of the house.

"What the hell is wrong with you. I had your back when that woman had a rifle to your head. You need to have mine."

I continued to the truck. I still wasn't sure if she'd had just cause when she shot the woman. Miami-Dade had let her slide with just a statement and she had only received probation from Martinez. If there had been any further administrative action—I wasn't aware of it. With a small smile, I opened the door of the truck for her, waited for her to get in, and closed it. Walking around to the driver's side, I glanced back at the house and saw the silhouette of Amos with a dog at each side looking out at us through the huge living room windows. It seemed as if this had been all staged, but I wasn't sure by whom.

I warned her to stay put for a minute and left her in the passenger seat. Justine was standing several feet away. "I'm so sorry, I have to drive her."

"I get it. You want me to take her truck?"

"You okay with that?"

"Heck no, I've still got your lips on my mind," she said.

I breathed, thanking whomever that my night was not totally

ruined. "Hold on." I walked around to the passenger window and asked Susan for the keys. Even she knew she couldn't, or shouldn't drive and handed them to me. I walked back to Justine and not caring if Susan saw or not, leaned in and kissed her.

"I'll follow," she said, and walked to Susan's truck.

I waited until she was right behind mine before I got in. Together we started back toward the glow of Miami.

After a few miles, Susan started fidgeting. "You want to tell me what happened in there?" I asked, wanting to get her take before the alcohol wore off and she could plan her statement.

"It's called investigative work, Hunter," she said bitterly.

I knew it was better not to respond and let her continue.

"He murdered that man and threw him in the cooling canal to make it look like FP&L had killed him. Then he did the same to his own sister."

I already suspected that FP&L was being set up for something, but there was nowhere near enough evidence to accuse Amos of anything—yet.

"You saw what he did to me. He's a killer."

"I'm going to forget, for your benefit more than his, whatever happened in that house tonight. It looks bad, Susan. Maybe we should drop it and regroup tomorrow."

"Sexual assault is not something to forget about."

I almost said that it could run both ways. As was the style these days, she had clearly set him up. I had an argument running through my head about how there were no witnesses or any way to corroborate her story, but it was not worth my breath. She knew what she had done. With the string of accusations running around about Washington and Hollywood elites misbehaving, it was almost too easy to point your finger at someone.

There was something else bothering me. "He sent the SOS text, didn't he?"

She rested her head against the window and closed her eyes. That was all the confirmation I needed and now I knew that besides a murder to solve, I had a partner I needed to watch very closely.

18

JUSTINE and I watched Susan fumble for her key. Finally, when we were about to help her, she let herself into her townhouse. A light went on and I decided that was as much as I needed to worry about Susan tonight. Tomorrow, I would have to deal with what she had done.

Dropping back into the driver's seat, I glanced over at Justine sitting next to me. She still had the key to Susan's truck in her hand. It was not worth the risk of giving her the means to do something else stupid tonight. I had thought about taking her phone as well. She probably had a personal vehicle, but I could only go so far to protect the world.

"You're special," I said to Justine, as I pulled out of the parking lot.

She slid closer. "That's just because I get off on dead bodies and special agent stuff."

"Well that too, but really," I said.

We held hands in a comfortable silence as I drove back to the headquarters building. A half hour later we had completed the commute to Adams Key.

I tried to be stealthy, and if I were alone, would probably have succeeded. The docking operation went well, but Zero must have sensed Justine was here. The screen door banged open and he came barreling toward us.

The smile on Justine's face as she bent down to pet him was the biggest I had seen all night. I wasn't sure if this was a good or bad thing, but if she was alright after what we had just seen, I was good with that. The lights were off in Becky and Ray's house, so I figured I had two guests for the night. During the day, we locked our homes when we were gone because of the tourists frequenting the picnic benches and shade structures. Adams Key was one of those rare places that was safer at night. This time of year, it was comfortable enough to sleep with the windows and doors open.

Zero followed us to my door, wagging his stubby tail and looking like he had accomplished his goal. Justine followed us in and I turned to her only to find the dog working his way between us. After receiving sufficient attention from both of us, he allowed us in the door.

"Beer?" I asked.

"You bet." She followed me into the kitchen with Zero on her heels. She opened the refrigerator and grabbed two beers. "Hey, you went fishing without me?"

"No," I said, moving by her side. I took the offered beer and twisted off the cap. Looking inside the refrigerator, I saw what she was referring to. Two packages of fresh fish sat on a plate. "Becky must be looking out for me. At least we've got breakfast." There weren't any supermarkets out here and though I usually mixed a shopping trip in with my land-based duties, I hadn't had time since I'd found the body.

We sat close to one another on the couch. Zero sighed heavily and dropped between our feet. Within seconds he was snoring and we shared a laugh at his expense.

"So, about your rogue agent?" Justine stated the question I had been thinking about.

"It's bad. I feel sorry for her."

"Sorry I doubted you. She really is everything you've said."

I looked down. Justine had thought I was being paranoid when I had first started working here. Among other things, Susan had used the GPS devices on the boat and in the car to track me. That had led to what I, and apparently the park service administration, saw as the unnecessary shooting she was now on probation for. She'd fired my gun the other day at the protest and her escapade tonight would only add another nail to the coffin if we decided to report it or Amos filed a complaint. She was likely out of a job. At her age, the only option open would be security guard. Even though the image of her sitting in a small room watching surveillance cameras and eating donuts kind of appealed to me, it didn't make me feel less sorry for her.

"What do we do about what just happened? I'm not thinking Amos is in a position to file a complaint. Should I just ignore it?"

She shrugged. "Are you really sure you saw what you think you saw?"

"Sexual harassment has become a tool. Sure, it's a horrible thing and should never happen, but it's a bad deal these days with people getting their lives ruined over accusations that are unprovable. And this 'me too' phenomenon only makes it worse."

"Let it slide. Even if she was setting him up it's not like he's an innocent victim. Amos is a big boy. They were at his house, drinking his whiskey. There were no witnesses."

"True," I said, taking a long sip of beer to change the subject. "You're off tomorrow, what do you want to do?"

"I don't have my board and the water temperature's a little cold for snorkeling. Want to go fishing?"

"That'd be cool." It was the answer I wanted. The tide chart that now resided in my head was in our favor as well. The best fishing would be around ten in the morning. Plenty of time for some early morning indoor activities. We finished our beers and headed off to bed. Zero woke up long enough to follow us to the bedroom, where he again collapsed on the floor and was snoring away before we finished brushing our teeth.

Zero woke me just after sunrise. My dreams of a lazy morning in bed were shattered by his nails clicking on the tile floor, and his persistence to be let out. He disappeared as soon as I opened the door. I turned back to the kitchen where Justine stood in the doorway rubbing sleep from her eyes.

"Breakfast? I'm famished," she said, opening the refrigerator and pulling out the fish.

She sautéed the fillets, tossing in whatever meager vegetables I had that had nothing growing on them. We ate, and an hour later were out the door. Though not as bad as the last few days, there was still a bite to the air. The wind was only around ten mph, but still out of the north, making it dry and cold. A small front must have passed through overnight. It hadn't brought rain like the one earlier this week, but the air was crisp and clear, much like California.

The weather might have been nice, but I had learned that even a quick three or four degrees drop in air temperature could put the fish off. Thinking about where to go, I guessed the power plant was still the best option. I thought for a minute about taking another look at the canals, but when I saw Justine coming toward me, I dropped all thoughts of work.

A nice Sunday usually filled the waterways and today, despite the proximity of Christmas (or maybe because of it), there were boats everywhere. I chose not to stop at the power plant. There were too many boats, and the charter captains were conspicuously absent. It was either too busy for them here, or the bite was better elsewhere.

I could feel Justine brush against me as we both studied the chart plotter looking for a better spot. The tide was wrong for the barrier islands where I had seen fish lately and I examined the screen, looking for inshore opportunities.

"We need something protected from the north wind with some flats and potholes. The sun should warm the water pretty soon and the fish'll come up out of the channels." We talked about several options until she found a good spot.

"Looks like we can get out of the wind here," she pointed to a small cove south of Card Bank."

"Might be good. The water's shallow enough and protected. Could be a good spot."

I pushed down on the throttle and we were soon up on plane,

cruising south toward the narrow gap through the Card Bank. This was the beginning of the hundred-and-twenty-mile stretch of the Keys, at least as they were recognized on maps. Geologically, the Keys extended from some twenty miles north of Key Largo through the entire length of the park and seventy miles west of Key West in the Dry Tortugas.

Approaching a gap in the Bank, I slowed and easily navigated the narrow channel through the shallows. Once we hit the other side, we idled to a small cove on the right. Two boats were already in the area, neither of which I recognized. They were rafted together, and I could tell from their reaction on seeing the park service boat that there was something going on here.

The southern bay was isolated, and aside from the one marked channel, required some local knowledge to navigate. A couple of miles across the water was North Key Largo, an interesting mix of wildlife refuges, developed areas, and abandoned developments. Whatever the two boats were doing, they were here for the privacy.

"You gonna go Ranger Rick on them?" Justine whispered over the idling engine.

I looked at her and saw the sparkle in her eye. Under normal circumstances with a civilian onboard, I would have called it in and taken off. Justine was different. As an employee of the Miami-Dade police department, she was not a civilian, and I had been in several situations with her and knew she could handle herself. Slowly, I idled into the deep-water section of the small sound as though we were looking for a fishing hole. Glancing over at us, the occupants of the boats, five men from the look of them, were still wary.

"You gonna let'em go?" Justine asked.

"Nope, just playing possum."

Running over there and pointing a gun at them was not going to get answers. From the look of the boats, they were a commercial mullet boat and a crabber; both wooden and in need of paint. Their captains and crews would be experienced at whatever they were doing. I skirted an area of coral heads and widened the circle. A quick glance showed several of the men were clearly watching us. It was my turn to be wary now. They must have been in the middle of something or they would have already taken off.

Reaching into the glove box, I pulled my gun from the holster and left it within easy reach. I was about to move closer when I heard a loud splash next to one of the boats. Turning to look, I saw two men fighting something in the water. I would have thought they had a fish, but there were no poles visible. Their engines, already running at idle, suddenly increased in volume and the boats took off.

The park service mandate was to protect the resources of the park, not to police anglers and hunters. That was for the Fish and Wildlife Commission. Thinking they were poaching, I reached for my phone and called the local dispatcher, reporting what I had seen and giving her our position. After reassuring me that they were on the way, I had a decision to make. With Justine aboard, I was not going to pull them over and possibly place her in danger. Instead, I decided to follow. "Can you get the registration numbers off them?"

The boats went in opposite directions and I saw Justine strain to see the small black numbers. Finally, she took her phone and entered them. The mullet boat heading south would be quickly out of our jurisdiction, so I took off after the northern-bound crabber. Following another boat is a lot harder than tailing a car. Boats tend to want some space and look badly at anyone encroaching on them—especially if the pursuing vessel has park service decals on the hull. There are no corners, alleys, or side streets to lose someone on the water, though, which makes it easier to follow from a distance

I had found taking obtuse angles was the best way to pursue another vessel without alerting them. The crabber headed through the narrow pass by the western shore, so I headed out toward the barrier islands. By using the main, marked channel, I was not as threatening, but could still clearly see the outline of their boat against the mangroves. Justine gave me a questioning look, and I explained to her what my plan was. She seemed satisfied.

We passed the last marker and entered the main bay. The crabber was still visible against the shore when, suddenly, it disappeared to the south of the cooling canals. I had noticed a small opening in the mangroves there, but it was overgrown and I didn't know where it led.

Now that the crabber was out of sight, I cut straight toward where it had disappeared, hoping they didn't have a lookout. As we approached, I could see mangroves extending out to a small point blocking the view from inside the channel. I steered toward the spot and, once I was a hundred yards off-shore, cut the engine down to an idle and motored slowly toward the mangroves. I didn't want either the engine noise or the inevitable wake of a fast-moving boat to alarm them.

There was no need to conceal my purpose now and I reached into the glove box for my pistol and belt. Checking the chamber, I put the belt on and holstered my weapon as we approached the narrow opening.

19

I COULD FEEL Justine tense beside me as we rounded the corner and entered the canal. Though I'd never been here, I knew we were in trouble once I saw the dead straight channel of water. There were plenty of cuts and passes through the mangrove islands here, some natural and some man-made. The difference here was immediately apparent. There were no overhanging mangroves or subtle bends to mask our approach. The view was almost a quarter mile of uninterrupted water.

We looked at each other. There was nowhere to go, but the crabber had disappeared. As we coasted forward, I shut down the engine to see if we could hear anything. Nature spoke back with the sound of fish jumping and birds chirping, and I thought I heard the grunt of a crocodile. There were no man-made noises.

"What the hell? They have some kind of cloaking device or something?" Justine whispered.

I put my finger to my lips and listened. The sound of an engine carried across the water. It was faint, and as it came closer the frequency told me it was not the crabber. The tin-can muffler on the off-road vehicle was loud and abrasive. Because it was water cooled, an outboard, even an old two-stroke one, was quieter. Scanning the shoreline, we watched for any sign of it.

Thankfully, it hadn't rained in a few days and the dryer, less humid air, had allowed the dirt to dry just enough to kick up a dust trail behind the vehicle, making it easy to see as it approached. I removed my gun from the holster and left it on the leaning post between us, then started the engine. The noise of the vehicle approaching would mask its sound. The question still remained, where had the crabber gone, but I suspected that answer would be found by tracking the UTV.

Slowly, I idled forward, with the northern bank on our starboard side. The vehicle was coming from that direction, and I was counting on the height of the bank to help conceal us. I handed the wheel over to Justine and hopped up on the gunwales. Leaning over the T-top, I loosened the ratchet attachments at the base of the two antennas and dropped them to horizontal. The reception would suffer significantly by reducing the line of sight they relied on, but we were within a mile of the headquarters building, and I guessed if we needed to make a call on the VHF radio it would reach. If not, we had our cellphones.

The T-top was still a problem, but there was nothing I could do about that except to rely on the angle of the bank. It was probably not uncommon for fisherman to try their luck here, so the boat by itself wouldn't look out of place. Park service boats were pretty nondescript. The only telltale markings were the green fabric on the T-top and decals on the hull.

The UTV slowed and the trail of dust died about a hundred yards away from the canal. Staying tight to the bank, I idled toward it thinking it was a dead end, but then, out of nowhere the canal showed a right-hand turn. This too was man-made, and as I entered, I shrugged at Justine. I guessed we were both wondering what we had gotten into.

South Florida is crisscrossed with a network of canals mostly dredged years ago, before the environmentalists put a stop to it. Some allowed boat access to the Intracoastal Waterway, others were cut to drain the swamp—allowing development to move further into the

Everglades. Many were abandoned and, like the mangrove-covered Keys, ideal for nefarious activities.

Justine saw my look and pulled out her phone. I wondered what she was up to and slowed. A minute later she slid closer, allowing me to see the screen. It was a satellite image of the area we were in with a blue dot showing our exact position. The canal ran straight as an arrow for about a half-mile and then stopped abruptly. Just in front of us was something strange. A square shaped peninsula with a pond was carved out of the terrain by two canals, one on either side. The right turn ahead was the first entrance. Judging from the area where the UTV had stopped, I guessed they were on the backside of it and the crabber was likely there as well.

"You want to call for backup?" Justine asked.

I had thought about it, but wasn't sure who to call. This was my territory and though it looked suspicious, I hadn't really witnessed a crime. The area was isolated. From the glance at the satellite image Justine had showed me, there were no real roads close by. Getting Miami-Dade to back us up would be impossible. Even if they had off-road capabilities, it would probably take a while to get them here. And I didn't think we were in helicopter territory yet. Besides, that would look bad on Martinez's balance sheet.

Chances were this was either a smuggling or poaching operation we were looking at. Johnny Wells, my buddy who worked for ICE was an option, but he ran a 39' Interceptor that needed a whole lot more water than the three feet we sat in. FWC was my next choice, but I was hesitant to call their dispatch number, wary of dealing with an unknown agent. Many of the FWC folks were just license checkers and several went no further than camping out in the channel leading to Bayfront Park where they randomly checked boaters on their way in. I didn't mind calling them for suspect activity I saw out on the water, but we were hemmed in with too many unknowns here. I had run across one of their agents several times in the park and he had seemed friendly.

"Can you look up Pete Robinson in my contacts?" I asked Justine. I wanted to keep my eyes on the shoreline.

"Sure," she said, grabbing my phone and entering our shared password.

"Ask him to meet us over here. Maybe some poachers for him."

She pressed the contact and waited. I thought it had gone to voicemail, but then he must have answered. Justine explained where we were, taking the GPS coordinates from the chartplotter.

"He says it'll take him about thirty minutes and maybe we should call the main office."

"We're not going to get another shot at this. At least he knows where we are."

She nodded. "You going in there?"

"It's the only way. You good with that?" I had already decided I would pull the plug if she was nervous.

"Yup."

I breathed in deeply and put the boat in gear hoping this was not a mistake and counting on the engine of the UTV covering the sound of my outboard. As we travelled into the cut, the mangroves started to thicken as we neared the end of the first canal alleviating my concern about the T-top's visibility. The channel was less than a hundred yards long and I could see the end. It was empty. Whatever was taking place was across the way.

Knowing the lay of the land a little better made my next decision easier. Entering the second canal without backup was crazy, with the crabber and UTV both there. The off-road vehicle could easily escape, but the crabbers would be trapped and likely fight their way out, especially once they saw it was just the two of us. I asked Justine to grab the rifle strapped to the bulkhead inside the console. At least we would each have a weapon. I nosed the bow toward the bank.

"I'm going to cross and see what they're up to," I said, going forward.

"Be careful."

"Just want to have a look." I climbed over the bow and turned to face the boat. After sinking to my knees in the mud yesterday, I had no plans to jump. Instead, I eased myself down, relieved to find firm footing.

It was too solid to be natural and as I started across the peninsula, I realized that it must be an abandoned development. Making waterfront property like this had been big business when it was allowed, but the Depression and subsequent storms delayed any construction until finally it was outlawed. Many isolated properties like this one, still remained.

The lake I had seen on Justine's phone appeared on my left. As I skirted its northern bank, I could see it had been dug for the fill I was walking on. Many of the subdivisions built throughout the state were still built in the same manner. It was only a couple hundred feet across the island and I quickly passed the pond and found a neglected road, probably the one used for the excavation equipment. Crossing it, I could see the canal through the brush and moved forward more cautiously.

Approaching the edge of the mangroves, I lowered myself into a crouch and started through the dense vegetation. It made for good camouflage, but the footing turned into a nightmare of tangled roots and muck. Using the little cover available, I tried to stay out of the water, moving from tree to tree until I could see the crabber.

It was pulled up against the far bank with one of the power plant's UTVs parked on the gravel bank adjacent to it. Three men stood there talking and I recognized one immediately. Bob, the security guard was handing over an envelope to one of the men from the crabber. I reached for my phone to use the camera only to find I had left it on the boat. There was no time to go back for it. Whatever was going down was happening right now.

The man took the envelope and signaled to someone on the crabber. A few minutes later two men appeared carrying a cloth bundle. Whatever was in it wiggled and squirmed making it difficult for the men to control. I had an idea what it was, but wasn't sure until I saw the reptilian tail. Even with its head covered and legs restrained they struggled with it until they were finally able to roll the bundle over the rail and into the bed of the UTV. Visibly relieved, they returned to the boat and I watched Bob and the captain talk like old friends for another minute. The casualness of the whole operation told me that they had done this before.

Bob called out a thank you to the crew, shook hands with the captain and went back to the UTV. I didn't wait. Working my way out of the mangroves, I reached dry land and ran back to the boat. I heard the high whine of the off-road vehicle as it sped away and, just as I reached the boat, heard the crabber's engine sputter and start. I Hoped that there was still enough time and that the sound of the UTV would cover my retreat, I hopped aboard and took the helm.

Starting the boat, I jammed the throttle into reverse and pulled off the bank. I used too much power and the engine scraped the mangroves behind me. The cowling was scratched for sure, and I cursed under my breath. Unless this turned out well, I would have hell to pay with Martinez. Without turning, I pushed the throttle forward and sped out of the canal. Too late, I pulled back on the lever in an attempt to slow the boat, but its momentum had already carried it into the sharp left-hand turn. With no way to stop, I stood paralyzed as the boat crabbed across the canal and smacked the far bank. Justine cried out, and I heard fiberglass crack; a sound I knew too well. Martinez would be all over me for damaging the boat, but there was no time to worry about him now.

It took a long minute to untangle the branches from the tower and I could only hope the propeller had not become caught between the far-reaching roots of the mangroves. It really didn't matter, there was no chance of getting out of here without being seen.

"They're right behind us," Justine called out.

Moving back to the helm, I jammed the throttle forward, tore out a section of branches, and headed toward open water. It was anything but graceful, but I stopped counting style points when I heard the first shot.

20

I PULLED Justine down to the deck just as a shot hit the Plexiglass windshield. Glancing up, I saw a spider web and hole where the bullet struck the impact resistant glass leaving a reminder for me of what was behind us. Reaching up, I pushed the throttle forward to its stop. The stern dug in, causing the bow to raise and block my sight, but after several seconds the hull was skipping across the top of the small wind-blown waves and I was able to see what lay ahead. I heard another shot and risked a glance back at the crabber. We both knew they couldn't catch us, not that they wanted to, but they had to guess we had seen the exchange. They fired another round before I saw the captain cut the wheel to starboard and head back to the south bay.

Justine was on the phone yelling instructions to Miami-Dade dispatch to send a helicopter after the crabber and I was forced to make a decision: follow the crabber or see where Bob was taking the crocodile. If the crabber was able to reach cover before the chopper arrived, the boat could be found through its registration number which Justine had already recorded in her phone. I suspected I knew where Bob was heading, and with the live crocodile in the back of the UTV, something bad was about to happen.

"We have to get back to headquarters and find him," I yelled over the roar of the engine. Cutting the wheel to port and away from the crabber. I crossed through the longer channel leading into Turtle Point between the #13 and #14 markers in four feet of water. The boat drew a little over two when it was on a plane and I used that to my advantage as I cut the corner of the marked channel to Bayfront Park. I hated to do it as other boaters watched what I did and some of them would figure that if it was good enough for the park service boats, they too could ignore the navigational aids as well. The problem was that they often misjudged what I had done, or didn't account for the tide. The same boaters wouldn't fail to report that they had followed what a park service boat had done when they grounded. With Martinez's ability to track me, I was sure I would hear about any complaint.

I was getting anxious and when I felt Justine place her hand over mine on the throttle, I released my death grip and backed off the speed just enough to avoid another boater. I knew she was right, but with Bob out there with the crocodile, I knew every second might count.

It was times like this that I wished I had a light bar. The other boaters affected by our wake stared at us, but they finally moved to the side of the channel when they saw the park service decal on the hull. We entered the turning basin, but were still coming into my slip too hot. There are no brakes on a boat, so I slammed the throttle to reverse to keep the bow from crashing into the concrete dock. The abrupt change in power caused the stern to fishtail into the port-side piling. The rub rail did its best, but I had overreacted, and winced when I heard the fiberglass scrape against the pole. I guess it didn't matter. There was already too much damage to conceal from Martinez. My only hope to escape his wrath, was to find the croc and catch the killer.

Thankfully it was Sunday and Martinez's cameras might be working, but the odds were that he was out playing golf. Scanning the parking lot, I saw no sign of Susan either.

"Come on," I called to Justine as I hopped onto the dock, and tied off the stern line while she handled the bow. With the boat secured, we ran for the truck.

It wasn't until we were rolling that I could explain my fear. Another murder was coming and my guess was that the target was Amos. From what I had just witnessed, Bob had to be involved, but from my recollection of our previous meeting, I didn't think he was working alone. That didn't matter right now. If the killers were moving up the organizational chart of MACE, Amos was next. I wasn't sure why they were killing the activists, but I did know how.

"Where are we going?" Justine asked as we turned onto SW 328th Street and headed west toward the Turnpike.

"It's got to be Amos. First the lawyer, then his sister. There's no place else to go except up. He's the top of the food chain." I realized the bad pun after it was out of my mouth.

"So, FP&L is going off the rails and killing the activists? That seems a little radical for a corporation."

"I don't think their board is sponsoring it. But someone is trying to make a statement." Something was percolating in my head, but it wasn't fully formed. Getting rid of the activists by demonizing the crocodiles didn't appear to serve any purpose. Without the crocodiles, it would be that much easier to close the plant. That was clearly not what FP&L wanted. I went back to the list of original motives for murder and tried to find one that fit the crimes and tried to find something out of place. It came to me in a flash of light.

"There's no other plausible solution." I explained my theory to Justine. She was about to respond when we heard something that sounded like several airplanes taking off simultaneously. To my left, the monstrous Homestead-Miami Speedway rose from the stark landscape. Cars and trucks were parked off the side of the road and I remembered the semis pulling the race cars in the other day. As we passed, I could see the top of the arena, packed to the last row.

"Rebecca?" Justine asked, when we were far enough away that we could resume our conversation.

"Rebecca." I was sure of it now.

"Not that I'm upset about losing some competition, but why?"

"Ambition." Number four on my list of motives. Sex was sexier, but I had seen her in front of the cameras. I thought back to the protest. She had been ready with a change of clothes and had a speech already prepared. "She's using this as a stage. Maybe with Amos's help."

"Then why murder Adrian?"

"She must have found out. Now I think she's gone off the rails and is after the last loose end—Amos."

We reached the Turnpike and I headed north toward Amos's house. "Can you try and find a number for him? Maybe call Grace Herrera. I think she interviewed him."

She turned her nose up at the mention of the name, but picked up her phone and called Miami-Dade dispatch. Several minutes later she was connected with Herrera and explaining my theory. Whether she was skeptical of my claim or not, she couldn't ignore it and promised she would call in backup. Justine dialed the number for Amos and put it on speaker. We both held our breath as the electronic ringer sounded five times and then looked at each other when it went to voicemail. I accelerated.

At least the park service truck had a light bar and although it was small, I decided it was time to use it. Surprisingly, the other motorists complied, and I caught some surprised looks when they saw who the vehicle belonged to. I ignored them and sped toward highway 41, turned west, and entered the Everglades.

Justine tried Amos's number one last time before we lost reception. Again, the call went directly to his voicemail. Fifteen minutes later, we turned into his driveway. I wasn't sure what I expected. There were no FP&L trucks blocking him in the house, and the place looked empty. Just as we got out of the truck a Miami-Dade cruiser appeared.

Introductions were quick, and after pleading with Justine to stay behind, the officer popped the trunk of the cruiser and handed me a bulletproof vest. I felt the added security the minute it was strapped to my chest, and as we headed toward the house we decided that since I was acquainted with Amos, that I would knock on the front door while the two officers checked the back.

I could hear the dogs barking inside, but no one answered. After several attempts with the doorbell, I knocked hard with the butt of my gun. Still nothing. Staying close to the house, I moved to the large windows and looked inside. Every room was empty. I wasn't sure whether to be relieved or more concerned when the Miami-Dade officers appeared shaking their heads. There was no dead body, which was a good thing, but also no Amos.

Justine joined us and after a brief conversation, the officers convinced me it would be employment suicide to break in. Nowhere in our search had we seen any evidence justifying a forced entry. After thanking them, we went back to the truck.

"What now?" Justine asked.

"Turkey Point. That crocodile was bought for a reason." I had wanted to warn Amos—now we needed to save him. "As soon as we get cell service you can call his office and see if he's there." He either wasn't the target or they had already taken him.

"His truck's not here either," Justine said.

I cursed under my breath because a forensic expert had just pointed out something I should have noticed immediately. Of course, they could have lured Amos somewhere else. Things were becoming murkier by the minute, but I had to go with my gut.

As we headed back toward the Turnpike and Turkey Point, I noticed the traffic coming toward us. It was just starting to thicken and when we exited on Palm Avenue it was gridlocked in both directions. We hit a standstill at the exit. My guess was the Speedway was letting out and it would only get worse. The time bomb in the back of the UTV was ticking in my head and I gripped the wheel tightly. Finally, we inched forward enough to see a Miami-Dade officer working traffic control. I opened the window and yelled to him.

"Turn your lights on and I'll get you past this mess," the officer called back.

He helped guide me through the traffic at the light and we inched past the lines of stopped cars heading the other way. This was taking much longer than I was comfortable with and I looked at my watch several times hoping time would stop—it had already been two hours since I had seen the crocodile tossed into the back of Bob's ATV. All I had done was waste time and drive in a big circle.

Justine pulled up a map on her phone and we turned right into a small subdivision. After a few blocks we were on a rough farm road. There are many roads like this in the area and we get five feet of rain per year, but either Martinez or someone above him had decided that we don't need four-wheel drive vehicles and I was paying for that cost saving measure right now.

The truck bounced and skidded along the rough crushed coral surface. We were jostled around the cab by the potholes and ruts, some still filled with water which scattered along the narrow surface like a minefield. It was impossible to steer anything close to a straight course with the hazards and I had to slow to five mph several times, wondering if we were going to make it out of some of the deeper potholes.

My fear came to fruition when within sight of the twin chimneys of the plant, I hit the mother of all potholes and the truck sank to its axle. There was no way out of this mess. Looking at each other, we grabbed whatever gear was available and started out on foot. Ignoring the sweat, which soon started to pour off my brow, I decided that this wasn't a bad idea. We were going as fast as we had been in the truck.

We reached the canals and started along the perimeter road. This was the same route that Bob had taken me on our tour and where I had seen the guards enter the system yesterday. I was alert now, my head on swivel, reacting to every sound. Justine stumbled and I grabbed her.

"A little jumpy there?" she whispered, wiping her brow as she recovered.

I realized that I had been startled when she tripped. I was clearly on edge and I needed to calm down. Though I was anxious about

Amos, I had to keep my emotions under control and rely on my training. The only problem was that Justine was with me.

This turned into less of a problem when my phone rang. For the second time in a critical situation, I had failed to put it on vibrate and it rang loud enough to startle some nearby birds. I looked at the screen. "It's Amos."

21

Before I answered the phone, I stared at the screen for a long second wondering how I had blown it. I hit accept.

"Detective?"

I was in no mood to correct him. "Hello, Mr. Androssa. We had a tip about another murder. Just wanted to check that you were okay." I didn't want to mention that the tip came from me.

"Thank you, Detective, but I am fine. Just enjoying a round of golf."

That explained why he wasn't home. I tried to envision Amos on a golf course, a hobby that seemed at odds with his environmental views. With their constant irrigation, abundant use of fertilizer and heavy equipment, the acres of grass were far from green. He must have sensed my unspoken judgment.

"It's quite the project. Eco Greens. Very green and sustainable. All the irrigation water is recycled. The equipment runs on biofuel and the fertilizer comes from farmed fish in the ponds."

I could tell he was excited about the project. I had to differ though. Having spent years in California I knew a little about green—and green wasn't always *green*. More water on golf courses was lost through evaporation than justified the cost of running the pumps to recycle the water. And I wished them luck running old French-fry grease through their equipment. "Just checking in then, enjoy your game."

We disconnected and I looked at Justine. "He's playing golf."

Our eyes caught and we laughed at our situation. "Nice date."

"Yeah," I didn't know what to do or say, but at least she was smiling. We did still have several problems. The park service truck was stuck on a back road in Homestead and there was also a hungry crocodile out there.

We had reached the access road to the canals. "There's no one out here," I said, scanning the canal system. The channels were over thirty miles long if you added them in total, but they fit into a ten square mile area. It seemed vast, but with the help of the flat terrain, you could see anything rising even a few feet from the ground. Even if you couldn't tell what it was, you could usually see movement.

"Wait. You said he was playing golf? Something about an Eco course?" Justine asked.

"He sounded pretty proud of it. Eco Greens, I think he said was the name of it." I wasn't sure where she was going with this.

"Golf courses have water holes and they have alligators. Where is this Eco Greens?"

I shrugged. He hadn't said. I pulled out my phone and looked it up in the maps app. Nothing came up in the search results, and I turned to Google. "The Keys Gate golf course." I read further. "It's an older course that closed. A developer bought it in 2014, but never did anything with it. It was sold again six months ago." I didn't need to know who bought it. Apparently, Amos was quite the businessman as well. Leaving the browser, I went back to the maps app and looked up the course by its old name. "It's right here."

Justine moved next to me. The course neighbored the cooling canals. Although they didn't have a common boundary, the two properties were separated by much of the same land we had just hiked. Perfect for Bob to run his UTV through and plant a crocodile in one of its ponds. "We gotta get over there." I started walking, but not toward the course. That would have required several miles of hiking, and we'd still have to find Amos once we reached it. Instead, I went toward the road leading to the plant's security office. First, I wanted to see if Bob was there and if he wasn't—I had a badge and meant to use it.

We'd come in at the northwest corner of the canals, which was also closest to the offices. It was still a half-mile slog, but faster than walking to the golf course. Ten minutes later, I wiped the sweat from my brow, and looked at the parking area. There were several UTVs parked as well as the standard security and personal vehicles. I couldn't tell from a casual glance which one of them Bob had used.

I pulled the door open and stepped back when the cool conditioned air hit my skin.

"Can I help you?" a man called out to us.

He was in the room with the monitors. Walking down the hallway, I responded. "Kurt Hunter, National Parks special agent."

"Oh yeah, didn't recognize you out of uniform. What can we do for you?"

I looked around the room, but there was no sign of Bob. "Is that guy around, the one that gave me the tour? I think his name was Bob." I was sure his name was Bob, but didn't want to set these guys on edge. They might be the ones I had seen fishing and hunting on the canals yesterday. I wasn't sure who was involved.

"No. He's out," he said.

This didn't look good and I needed a way to explain myself. "He seemed like a nice guy and I need a little help. Kind of embarrassing really."

I had his attention now and I got the feeling this was going to be water cooler talk for a while.

"What can we do for you, agent?" he asked, exchanging a conspiratorial look with the other guard sitting next to him.

"Well, me and my girlfriend were driving the back roads here and hit a pothole. Got the truck stuck. You were close so we walked over." I ate crow hoping it would put them off guard, yet not forgetting how close to the truth it was.

"Gotta watch them roads. That's why we have those UTVs out there. Not much we can do about the truck. Need a ride somewhere?"

It would cost me, but he had bought it. "There's some federal property in the truck. Being Sunday and all, there's no one working maintenance over at headquarters. I can't leave it overnight. Special agent stuff." I had to stop myself before I winked at him. "Maybe I can borrow one of those off-road things?"

They looked at each other deciding who was going to make the decision. I thought I could help. "Rebecca Moore said anything I needed...."

The mention of her name had an unusual reaction. It was like the air was sucked out of the room—Justine included.

"If Ms. Moore authorized you, I guess we can comply."

The man reached up and grabbed a set of keys off the board next to his desk and tossed them to me. Fortunately, I caught them.

"You need a lesson?"

"I'm good. Used to run one out west in the National Forest." I was more familiar with off-road vehicles than boats. "Appreciate your help. I'll get it back to you later." I made a move for the door before they called Rebecca or changed their minds.

"Watch out for them crocs out there. Dangerous buggers," one of the men said—and they both laughed.

I laughed along and Justine and I were out the door before they knew it. The key tag had a number that I matched to one of the UTVs. We jumped in, buckled the safety harnesses, and minutes later were flying over the gravel road. Justine took her phone out of her pocket and started navigating.

Fifteen bone-jarring minutes later the first fairway came into view and we sped toward it. Once we were off the gravel road and on the cart path, the ride leveled out and, not wanting to advertise our presence, I reduced speed. My first reaction to Eco Golf was how brown the course was. I had my doubts that this was the future of golf. The first three holes we cruised were deserted. There were no flags in the greens, if you could call them that. Martinez would have certainly turned up his nose.

Justine called out the hole numbers as we passed them. We had entered the course at the tenth hole and with the numbers climbing and no one in sight, I figured we were going in the wrong direction. I spun a U-turn, engraving a deep rut in the fairway where I went off the path. It wasn't the only one and I thought the locals might be using the course as their personal off-road area.

Backtracking, I increased speed and returned to the tenth hole where the course made a hundred-eighty degree turn for the clubhouse. The grass became greener as the numbers on the hole placards went down, and on the sixth green we spotted two lone players.

It wasn't hard to pick out Amos from that distance. Standing almost a head above the figure next to him, he leaned over to pick up a ball from the hole. He handed it to a woman standing nearby.

"That's her. Your FP&L lawyer girlfriend?" Justine said.

I squinted hard, having to work to recognize her, and wondered if Justine had some kind of female radar. "What's she doing out here with him? They're supposed to be enemies."

"It certainly doesn't look like it."

Walking to their cart together, Amos put his arm around Rebecca. She didn't pull away, but neither did she lean back into him. Their interaction confirmed my theory that they were in this together. I looked around for the other two members of the foursome and realized they were playing alone. In fact, I didn't see anyone behind them. Together they sped off toward the next hole—and us.

Even from a distance, Rebecca would recognize the FP&L vehicle and likely tell that its occupants were not employees. There was a slight bend in the road that allowed me a few seconds to make a move. Spinning another U-turn would take too long, so instead, I gunned the accelerator and yelled to Justine to hold on as the UTV roared cross-country onto the adjacent fairway. A grouping of palm trees used to separate the two fairways blocked their view long enough for me to climb the manicured grade and drop into the swale around a man-made pond.

An excavator and backhoe sat parked nearby. I spun around behind them and cut the engine.

"Do you think they saw us?" Justine asked.

"Hope not. But now what?" I asked the question more to myself than to her. "Can I see that satellite view?" She handed me her phone. There were a half-dozen lake-sized water features cut into the course. I tried to find our position relative to the remaining nine holes. A large dogleg lake was between the ninth and tenth holes. I remembered speeding past it earlier, not thinking it significant. Now it looked like a good place for a murder.

22

"Look," I zoomed in and showed Justine the lake. "It's gotta be there. They wouldn't even have to drive on the course to get the croc in position."

"So, they have the seventh and eighth holes to play before they reach the pond. That should give us time to circle around without being seen."

I was grateful for the respite even if it would only be a few minutes. Starting the engine, I pulled away from the equipment and headed perpendicular to the seventh fairway. I wanted to put some distance between us and the unlikely couple as well as create the opportunity to come in wide and surprise Bob.

We hit a perimeter road that I guessed from the tire tracks was used by the heavy equipment. Passing planted fields on the right, we followed the road around, not slowing until we reached the boundary of the tenth fairway. To access the lake from there we had to cross the brown grass. I wasn't worried about tearing up the course; others had done that already. The problem was that the fairway leveled out and I could see clear across to the depression where the pond was. Anyone I could see could also see me.

We still had the advantage of the FP&L vehicle until we were close enough to be identified. That should allow us to see what was happening. Neither Bob or Amos and Rebecca would immediately suspect it. Slowing more, I moved onto the path and drove toward the ninth hole.

The green was elevated a few feet, probably for drainage—it wasn't a lot, but I used it, cruising around the far end—to give us some cover. At the back of the hole we had a good vantage point and looking toward the lake, we saw Bob's UTV.

He was backed up to the water. The gate to the pick-up bed was open. "Can you get a video?" I asked Justine. She took her phone out and started filming.

"We need to get closer," she said. "You can't tell who it is."

"What about the zoom?" I asked, regretting it immediately—when she turned to me. There was no need for a response. Starting the UTV, I worked my way toward the lake, trying to use the undulating ground for cover. It wasn't much, and I decided the best route would be straight at him. I had no way of knowing if it was only the two of them or if there were more guards involved. Hopefully, he had co-conspirators and wouldn't recognize us.

"Better?" I asked. I'd go only as close as needed to get a clear video.

"It's going to be really grainy from here. We've got to get closer."

We had no choice but to go on foot. Driving any closer with the power plant's UTV would attract his attention and he would immediately know it was not one of his buddies. Seeing two people walking around a golf course would seem harmless enough. "We have to go on foot."

Justine agreed and I parked the UTV. We set out, walking as casually as possible toward the golf cart path that skirted the lake. Justine was still shooting video and I saw him look up. He was staring straight at us. "Act normal," I advised.

"Like any of this is normal?"

"Casual then." I was dressed in board shorts with my fishing shirt untucked, and had flip-flops for footwear. Justine had a bikini top and shorts. I could only hope the eco crowd had their own take on golf fashion, or that Bob was so preoccupied with the crocodile and his murder plan to notice. Just in case it would help I began tucking my shirt in.

"Is that a gun in your pocket or are you just happy to see me?" Justine looked at my sidearm now in plain view.

I untucked the shirt again. We were close to the tenth green now. It was in better shape and had more color than the brown greens we had recently passed. Several pieces of heavy equipment were parked off to the side. The crews must have been working in this direction.

I changed course and started walking faster to a backhoe. "We can use that to get closer." Reaching the machine, I climbed up on the steel step and opened the door to the operator's cab. As I'd expected, the keys were in the ignition. In general, there was little security for heavy equipment, as I had discovered while working a case back in the Plumas Forest. I had learned that there were only five keys made for all John Deere equipment, and they are readily available on the Internet.

"Come on." I extended my hand and helped Justine into the cab. There was only one seat, but enough room on the side without controls to accommodate her. She closed the door and I started the engine. Bob looked our way when he heard the loud diesel, but turned back unconcerned. It was the perfect disguise.

It took a minute to figure out the controls. I had driven many pieces of equipment and it came back quickly. Deere's were easy to run and soon we were bouncing down the hill toward the lake. I slowed when I felt Justine's grip on my shoulder. Moving a couple of hundred feet from Bob, I stopped by the water. "How's this?"

"Spectacular." She cracked the window and started shooting video.

"I can't just sit here," I said, backing up and turning around. I dropped the outriggers and raised the wheels off the ground. With the machine supported, I spun the seat a hundred-eighty degrees to operate the excavator, extended the boom, and dropped the bucket to the waters edge. I looked back at Bob, who was ignoring us, and took a scoop of mud from the shore. I swung the boom to the side and dumped it on solid ground. Trying to look like this was my job, I continued to pull material from the lake.

"He's pulling the bag from the bed."

Running the equipment took all my attention and I was relying on Justine's running commentary to know what Bob was doing. The video would be helpful as evidence, but would not stop the murder. I needed to take action. The bucket reached into the lake and I pressed the thumb switch on the toggle control. I was rewarded with a full scoop of mud that I dumped to the side. Bringing the boom in, I retracted the bucket and swung back around. After lifting the outriggers, I pulled forward, switching to four-wheel drive to help move the big tires over the soft ground.

If not for the crocodile just released into the lake this almost could have been fun. I turned toward Bob's UTV and watched as he sped off. There was really no choice now.

With no one watching I used all the speed the machine had to reach the release spot. Justine grabbed onto me as we bounced along the uneven grade by the shore. Once a piece of equipment this large starts bouncing, the only way to control it is to stop, but I needed to find the croc before it had a chance to swim off. We reached the tire tracks left byBob's UTV, exited the cab, and hopped down to the ground. I glanced in the direction that Bob had taken off and saw no sign of him. But something caught my eye moving toward us. A golf cart come into view. Amos and Rebecca were about to tee off on the ninth hole. In a few minutes, they would be on the green and in range of the crocodile.

I had no idea how Bob planned to execute the murder with a loose croc, but I had to assume he had a plan. The only way to stop the murder was to stop the croc. Panning the water I looked for the telltale sign of its brow, backbone, or tail. "We have to find it," I said, straining my eyes.

"There," Justine said, pointing to a small hump by the bank.

I pulled out my gun and started toward it.

"What are you doing?"

"There's nothing else we can do. Amos and Rebecca will be here any minute."

The only problem with my plan was that the shot would alert Bob as well as the twosome that something was wrong. I didn't have a silencer, but knew there was a way to do it. "Get me that plastic bottle from the cab," I called to Justine. Working my way into position, I watched the crocodile.

My heart was pounding and I could feel the blood pumping in my ears. The crocodile was only twenty feet away and could easily attack and kill me. I realized why Bob had gone through the trouble of paying the crabber to poach a wild crocodile now. The hatchlings from the cooling canals were all tagged. Not only did that make them identifiable, but also growing up in their protected environment with an overabundance of food, they weren't afraid of people.

Justine handed me the empty juice bottle and gave me one of her looks. It would take longer to explain than to do the deed. Removing the cap, I jammed the plastic end over the barrel of the gun, thankful that the mouth of the juice bottle was wide enough. We'd done this with 22 rifles and 2-liter soda bottles in the woods back home and I hoped it would work with the louder 40 caliber I carried. Raising the gun, I tried to aim, but the bulk of the bottle obscured the sights. I could feel the pounding in my ears as I inched closer.

When I was ten feet away, I raised the gun again. Before I could pull the trigger, the crocodile must have sensed me and with a loud splash spun away. I took the shot I knew I didn't have, and saw the wake of the animal already moving ahead of where the bullet had splashed. At least the silencer had worked. Staring at the water looking for the crocodile, I hoped for another chance when Justine pointed it out.

"Too far. I might have a chance without the silencer, but . . ."

"If we move by the bank over there, we have a clear view of the ninth green and the lake. At least we can see how they're going to pull off the attack and be in a position to stop it."

I followed her, knowing it was the best chance we had—though it had its own problems. For one, we would have our backs to either the twosome or the lake. Either could prove deadly. We crept around the green, staying low. I pointed to a sand trap at the edge of the green with a steep bank carved into it. It would make it a difficult shot and hard to escape from, but it also provided the best cover I could see.

Staying low, we moved toward the bunker. I heard a plop as one of their balls hit the green and I started moving faster. Before I could locate the other ball, we were in place. Peering over the edge, I could see the cart coming toward us and I took an anxious look behind. At least since we were on a slight rise from the lake, we would be able to see the crocodile approach as it was lured to its victim.

Kneeling in the sand, I heard the sound of a gas powered vehicle approach. Electric golf carts were almost silent. I had to think it was Bob. Peering over the edge and then around us, I couldn't see him, but an engine was definitely coming toward us. I had to duck back down when I heard Amos say something to Rebecca. Looking back at the green, I saw them walking toward us.

They stopped at the furthest ball, which happened to be Amos's. He started to line up the shot. I turned when I heard something behind me. The crocodile was making its way up the bank. It was still a good distance away from the two golfers but moving quickly.

With my eyes still on the croc, I heard the tap of the ball and Amos cursing. Thinking he had made a bad shot, I kept my focus on the more immediate threat until I heard Rebecca.

"Can you help me check the lie of my ball?"

I took my eyes off the approaching crocodile and turned toward the green. Amos was following Rebecca toward her ball. Looking back at the water, I saw they were on an intercept course with the crocodile.

23

When the wind shifted it all came together. I could clearly smell the menhaden oil now. Bob must have laced the grass with it. I remembered Steve, the zoologist saying that alligators and crocodiles had poor vision but an excellent sense of smell. The crocodile had zeroed in on the scent and was now following it directly toward its next meal. The wind also brought the sound of the UTV with it.

Everything was coming together too quickly and I still wasn't sure who the good guys and bad guys were. Even though I could easily dispatch the crocodile from the sand trap—I had to wait. Shooting it now would expose us and give the murderer a reprieve. As they came closer, Rebecca seemed to take the lead. It appeared that she was asking Amos a question. It might have seemed innocent enough to Amos, but to me, it looked like a diversion.

"Look, the security guy's taking a set of clubs off the cart," Justine whispered, and pointed across the green.

I was so involved in watching the drama unfolding in front of us that I missed the UTV. Only one set of clubs remained on the driver's side. Bob had the other set, and was back in the UTV and heading our way.

With her club's gone, she was never here. Rebecca was clearly the brains. Unaware of our presence, Bob sped toward the edge of the green. Rebecca waved her hand as if she were expecting him. She turned and started walking in the direction the UTV was coming from. Amos seemed disinterested. He must have assumed it was some kind of urgent FP&L business she was being summoned to. Just then the sun came out from behind a cloud and I could see the slick grass where the menhaden oil had been applied. It started in a thick swath near the water and narrowed as it approached the kill zone at the edge of the green. This was well planned and orchestrated.

So far Bob had done all the heavy lifting. I just needed Rebecca to do one thing to confirm her part in this and I would shoot the croc and end it. It took all my patience and I wished I could give some to Justine who was starting to get anxious. Amos finally saw what was happening when Bob ran the UTV behind the croc urging it forward. Rebecca pushed Amos, knocking him down, and ran to the side of the green. The entire scene was staged to look like Amos was out alone, playing a round of golf when the crocodile had taken him. Even the presence of the crocodile this close to its natural habitat wouldn't be questioned. This late on a Sunday, there would likely be no one else on the already deserted course and the irrigation system would erase any traces of the menhaden oil used to lure the croc to the kill zone.

I had what I needed and rose from the sand trap with my gun extended. Amos was on his hands and knees wondering what was going on. The crocodile was only twenty feet away when I took the first shot. Just as the bullet left the barrel, the crocodile picked up speed. It took the hit behind the head in the fleshy part of its thick neck and continued. Amos was on his feet now and started running back to the golf cart, but it was pointless. In a short footrace the crocodile would win.

In a shooter's stance now, I tracked the croc and took another shot. This one pierced its head and I could only hope the thick bone protecting its brain had not slowed the bullet. The crocodile let out a loud grunt and dropped. Amos was oblivious and still heading to the cart. He was safe, and that was what mattered. I turned to where the

UTV had been and it was gone. I realized that while putting down the croc I had suffered a moment of tunnel vision.

"Where'd they go?" I asked Justine.

"Look," she said, pointing toward the golf cart.

I turned just in time to see Rebecca wind up and hit Amos in the head with a club. He staggered for a second and then before she could hit him again, fell to the ground. Bob and Rebecca went back to the body and together struggled to load it into the bed of the UTV. They hopped back in and took off.

We were too far away to get off a clear shot. I guessed that they were heading back to Turkey Point. Looking around, the backhoe was the closest mode of transportation. We'd never catch them in it, but it was faster than running back to where we had stashed the UTV. We ran to the backhoe and climbed in. As soon as the engine caught, I lifted the bucket overhead and jammed the lever forward. The machine reacted and lumbered up the bank. Once it reached the top I was able to shut off the four-wheel drive and our speed increased. We bounced across the dead grass of the tenth fairway to where we'd left the UTV.

"It's not there," I yelled over the diesel engine. I was pretty sure where I had left it, but then realized that Bob's course back to Turkey Point had probably passed right by it. There had been no reason for me to take the keys out, and Rebecca was probably following him back with it, leaving us nothing but the backhoe to chase them with.

Backhoes are not slow, but they can be uncomfortable when driven at speed across rough terrain. With no choice, that's what we did. Fortunately the enclosed cab was air-conditioned and Justine and I could talk. "Can you call Miami-Dade and get some help?"

"Sure thing," she said and took my phone.

I followed in the general direction of the small dust trail from the two UTVs ahead, having to veer one way or another when I encountered an obstacle that the backhoe couldn't handle.

"They'll head this way, but we need to give them a location," Justine said, handing me back the phone.

When I turned to take it, I saw a yellow tow strap rolled up behind her. Looking forward, I saw the dust trail moving farther away and guessed the UTVs were traveling at roughly twice the speed of the backhoe. We'd never catch them. I made a quick decision and turned to the left.

"Where are you going? They're over there," Justine said.

"Back to the truck. We can't catch them, but with that tow strap behind you we can pull the truck out." It was a slight detour from catching up to Bob and Rebecca, but might be well worth the effort to have a real vehicle. Remembering the satellite shot from Justine's phone, there was only so far we could drive a UTV before we would need a road-worthy vehicle. Homestead Air Force Base would block any escape to the north and Card Sound Road provided a barrier to the south. To the east was the bay and the west the Turnpike. It was a large area, but they were still trapped.

I watched their dust trail disappear. I was confident with my new plan, but still regretted letting them out of my sight. It took several attempts aided by Justine and the image on her phone to find the gravel road, but finally the truck lay ahead. I'd towed many vehicles out of bad situations in the national forest. Within minutes I had the one end of the strap hooked to the truck's tow points and looped the other end of the strap over the bucket of the backhoe.

Justine was willing to drive, but backhoes take some finesse so I hopped back in the operator's seat and set the lever to reverse. Slowly the slack came out of the strap and the truck emerged from the hole. Jumping down to the gravel road, I unhooked it and gave the chassis a brief inspection. Aside from a coating of mud, everything looked alright and I signaled for Justine. We left the backhoe beside the road and hopped into the truck. I couldn't help but think it looked as bad as the boat. Martinez would be all over me tomorrow. Careful not to hit any more potholes, I retraced our way back toward a real road.

We reached a smoother road. It was still unpaved, but was well maintained. It also had a name allowing us to locate it on the map. At first glance Lucille Road looked like it ran to the power plant, but we ended up in a small turnaround just short of the first cooling canal. I had to turn and backtrack to SW 137th Ave.

We were on pavement now. After the bone-jarring ride on the rough gravel road, and across the uneven terrain in the UTV and backhoe, I was finally able to think. It took a few minutes to adjust my voice to the lower noise level in the pickup.

"What's the plan, Kemo sabe?" Justine asked.

I hesitated. Having been so focused on saving Amos to this point, I had none. "We've got to stop this. Let the District Attorney's office sort out the who did what and how to charge each of them."

"You think this ends with them?"

I wasn't sure, and said so. "Damn." I hadn't been watching the road and a hundred yards short of SW 344th Street we skidded to a stop behind a long row of brake lights. Ahead loomed the raceway which, from the look of the traffic, had just let out. I turned on the light bar hoping there was traffic control at the intersection and the officer would see us. It didn't seem to matter and we crept slowly along.

"That sucker holds 46,000 people," Justine said, quoting Wikipedia from her phone. "And they're all in front of us."

"If we can reach the intersection, it's a right turn. That should be against traffic."

"You've never been to a race before," she said.

I wasn't sure what she meant until finally, the officer working the intersection saw the flashing lights on the truck and motioned us through. I turned right hoping for a clear ride and quick arrests. I quickly learned what Justine was talking about. *Shit-show* was the only description that came to mind. Apparently all the spectators, hyped up from watching the race, thought they were race car drivers too. Horns blasted and engines revved, as they jockeyed for position to go nowhere, clogging both lanes in their effort.

I pulled off to the side of the road and while watching the danger ahead tried to decide what to do. We were at a disadvantage with the small park service truck only having two seats. Finding Amos and arresting Rebecca and Bob, would be problematic. "We need to call Miami-Dade. They need to do better than to be waiting for a location," I said.

"Guess Sunday is Kurt's potential girlfriend day," said Justine. "One's out since she's a murderess, I'll give detective Herrera a call and see how that turns out." She picked up her phone and dialed the secret Miami-Dade dispatch number that only employees had.

I knew she was kidding, but it still stung. I hoped I had done nothing to earn it.

"She's on the way with two cars. Said to wait here and they'll clear a path."

I wondered how that was going to happen. Looking at the scene ahead with the cars, pickups, and SUVs, all driven by wannabe Jeff Gordons made it look almost impossible. Our chance of saving Amos was getting smaller fast. Cursing myself for not calling for help sooner, we sat at the side of the road with nothing to do but worry and wait for Grace Herrera and Miami-Dade to save the day.

24

My patience level soon matched Justine's. She was ready to climb out of the truck and go after them on foot. It took more persuasion than I thought I was capable of to stop her. Finally, we heard the intermittent blast from the siren of the Miami-Dade cruiser. However, it was one thing to hear them and another thing for them to navigate through the post-race gridlock and reach us. Even if they did, there was nowhere to go.

"We're just wasting time. There's nothing they can do to help," Justine said.

I had to concur. "We're too far from anywhere to go on foot and have no idea where they went. We could be stuck here an hour."

"Okay, where would you go if you had Amos?" she asked.

It didn't take me long. "Scene of the crime."

"Then we'll go by boat," she said.

I was getting frustrated and was about to throw up my hands when I saw what she was looking at. Alongside the road ran a canal. Across the fifty-foot expanse of green water were two fishermen in a bass boat.

"We only need to get a few miles," Justine said, opening the door.

I only had a few moments to decide if this was a good idea or another pit I would have to crawl out of when Martinez found out I had commandeered a private boat. Stepping out of the truck, I climbed into the bed for a better look. Cars were still stacked up as far as I could see, blocking both lanes. With only a narrow gravel shoulder before the roadway disappeared into either the canals on one side or the brush on the other, there was no way the cruiser was going to reach us anytime soon.

I jumped out of the pickup bed and wove my way through the vehicles which were clogging the road to both sides. Calling out to the fishermen, I got a look, but no response. A minute later, Justine stood next to me and tried. One responded to her. Another minute later, and they had reeled in their lines and were motoring across the canal.

"Better let me do the talking," Justine said.

I told myself to deal with the bruise to my ego later and agreed. It was the end that mattered now, not how we got there.

"Hey, ma'am," one of the fishermen called to her.

I cringed at the insincerity of the courtesy.

"Any chance y'all would run us out to the bay?"

The two men looked at each other and talked for a minute. Finally, the one that had called out agreed.

"We was 'bout to call it a day. Got the trailer over at the park."

"That'll work, guys."

The boat approached the bank and I realized we would have to climb down the soft slope to reach them. "Careful. The footings pretty sketchy," I whispered to Justine.

She took off her flip-flops and easily descended the bank. I did the same, but not so gracefully and heard the banter from the fishermen when I fell. Scraping the dirt from my legs, I watched as both men moved to the bow to help Justine aboard. Neither extended the courtesy to me. Thankfully, the bass boat had a low freeboard and I was able to step onto the bow. But before I could reach one of the empty seats by the stern, the boat took off like a rocket. There were no rails on the low gunwale, so I grabbed the coaming and hung on.

Justine sat sandwiched between the men, who were too close and too friendly for my liking. I knew she was being flirtatious for the cause, but it still hurt to watch. The two-hundred-fifty horsepower engine had the lightweight boat up on plane in less than a hundred yards and eventually I was able to reach one of the seats by the transom. The banks flew by, and I guessed we were going somewhere north of fifty mph. The boat was probably half the weight of my park service center-console and had a hundred additional horsepower.

The ride to the bay was fast through the dead straight canal and we left the five-mile stretch of canal less than ten minutes later. The driver took a hard turn to port and the boat skidded as it lost purchase on the water. My stomach dropped as it rocked from side to side before it settled. I'd been at or close to this speed on Johnny Well's ICE Interceptor, but that boat had a deep V and was thirty-nine feet long. Now in open water every wave unsettled the lightweight hull and the bass boat was tossed back and forth. Thankfully, a few minutes later the driver turned hard to port again and we entered the channel to Bayfront Park and headquarters.

The goodbyes, at least those with Justine lasted too long, but she finally pulled away from the men. I was already on the dock moving towards my center-console. While I waited for her, I looked around the small marina trying to avoid boat envy. Both the FWC and ICE boats were far superior to mine.

I felt the center-console move. Justine stepped aboard and came toward me. I stood frozen in indecision. She had gotten us here, but now I wasn't sure what to do. There was a whole lot of water out there and Bob and Rebecca could be anywhere, including on the road. "Can you get the lines and then call Grace and have them keep an eye on the roads?"

She shot me an *I know what to do* look and picked up the phone. I tried to look confident while I waited for the engine to lower into the water. Once the pitch of the lift changed, I turned the key and started it, pulling back the throttle a little too fast and throwing Justine off balance.

She gave me another look and came beside me. Avoiding eye

contact, I stared down at the chart plotter like I had some kind of ESP that would tell me where the murderers had gone. In fact they could be anywhere, but I figured we had to start somewhere and the Turkey Point plant was the logical place. Justine was on the phone with Miami-Dade, calling in a BOLO on our suspects. I finished the turn and just before heading into the main channel, looked back at the dock. I don't know why I cared, but Susan's boat was in its slip. Tied up like she was waiting for a hurricane, it gave me at least some reassurance that she wasn't going to interfere.

Moving back to the current situation, I finally summoned the courage to look at Justine. "Good job with the rednecks," I said, offering some praise to smooth the tension.

"*De nada*. Miami-Dade has the BOLO out. It's still a shit show out there by the speedway."

"I'm going to head over to Turkey Creek and see if we can find them. They'd at least need to ditch the UTVs for a real vehicle."

"Makes sense."

I was saved from further conversation when we passed the last marker. I pushed down on the throttle and cut the wheel to starboard. Heading south toward the chimneys, I wondered how to handle what lay ahead and thought briefly about calling Martinez. A wave caught me off balance and tossed that idea from my head.

Approaching the small cove where I had docked the other day, I slowed to an idle and glanced around the corner. I wanted to take a quick look and make sure they had not returned the UTVs and headed out in a vehicle. There were no boats at the dock or anyone in sight. Feeling a little more confident that we would not be assaulted taking the beach, I pulled up to the dock and tied off the bow line. Checking my gun belt, I grabbed my phone and hopped onto the dock. Justine started to follow with the rifle from the console.

That was easier than I expected and without turning back, I walked to the end of the dock and started toward the security building. I was pretty sure there was no taking these two by surprise. They had seen me shoot the crocodile and knew that I had seen them.

Staying close to the adjacent building, I looked out at the parking lot. I didn't know how many UTV's the plant had, but there were two empty parking spaces. That probably meant that Bob and Rebecca had never returned. They had murder on their minds—not escape.

25

IF THAT WAS what their game was, I needed help and now. They had enough of a head start that the deed might already be done. The only hope I had that Amos was still alive were the missing UTVs. We needed to get out to the cooling canals, but with ten square miles to cover, an aerial assault was the fastest way to locate them and that meant calling in Miami-Dade.

"Can you get a helicopter?" I asked Justine.

"Poof." She moved her hands like she could summon one with fairy dust.

I waited impatiently for the call to go through. Even with her super-secret number, the request was passed up the chain of command. Finally, she turned to me with a frown.

"They're going to need someone higher up to authorize this."

I extended my hand for the phone. "This is Special Agent Hunter."

My ego took another blow when the dispatcher told me clearly that unless we had first hand knowledge, as in a visual of the suspects, there would be no reconnaissance mission. I disconnected and looked at Justine. She shrugged. I already knew there wasn't much she could do. It was up to me.

Dreading the call, I pulled my phone out and pressed Martinez's name. The call went through quickly and before I could weave my suspicions into an emergency his phone started to ring. I counted five rings and wasn't sure if I should be relieved or angry when it went to voicemail. I half listened to his recorded message as I tried to compose my own, when I heard Susan McLeash's name mentioned as the next in line to call if he was unreachable.

Now I was angry. He probably didn't answer because his phone was in his golf bag sitting on the back of his cart. Hearing Susan's name just put me over the top. Justine sensed it and looked at me, but I stared through her, wondering what this was going to cost me. I pressed Susan's name in my contacts, knowing I had no choice if we were to save Amos.

Susan answered on the second ring. I could tell she wasn't sure how to deal with a call from me on a Sunday, especially after what had happened last night, and meekly said hello.

"I need you to authorize a chopper from Miami-Dade. Martinez's recording says you're the next in line."

Her tone changed instantly. "You in trouble, Hunter?"

I explained what had happened and what I suspected, hoping the cowgirl in her would come out and she would make the call. When I mentioned Amos's name though, I had a quick thought that she might also want him dead. As they say, dead men tell no tales. Her need for redemption and publicity took over.

"Give me a minute. What's your location?"

Her tone told me she was angling to take charge, but Amos was out there and I had to do something. I gave her all the information I had.

"Stay put. I'll make the call."

Slightly relieved, I put the phone in my pocket and turned to Justine. There was no way we were staying put. "Can you get the lines?"

"Not waiting for backup?"

"Nope. I fear we are already behind the curve here."

"I'll drive." She took the wheel.

Justine was a better and more aggressive driver than I was. I had no problem turning over the boat to her and went to the bow where I removed the line. Before I could make it back to the helm, she had spun the boat and was heading out the channel. Running fast, she spun the wheel to starboard, and followed the shore around the plant to the outflow. I grabbed the seat and held on tightly as the boat bounced along the tips of the waves. A few minutes later, we were around the bend and looking at the bank containing the last canal.

The top of the berm was above eye level and I was unable to see past the embankment. Climbing onto the leaning post, I used the stainless steel supports for the T-top and started to climb it. Reaching the top, I braced my legs against the structure and scanned the canals. The additional five or six feet gave me a clear view of the nearer channels, but I saw nothing. I noticed the increased temperature and humidity had created a haze over the ground, reducing visibility.

"Can you check on the helicopter? Try channel seventeen." I took a minute to extend the antenna back into position. If Bob and Rebecca were out of sight, I doubted they would see or care about the thin white whip. The radio crackled to life, but it was only static. Just then my phone vibrated and I descended to the deck. It was Grace Herrera looking for any information. I gave her my position. Just as I finished I heard the helicopter in the distance.

Sitting there doing nothing was not in my DNA. It must not have been in Justine's either. Without warning she pushed the throttle forward, throwing me off balance and headed south. It was hard to believe it had only been a few hours since we were here. Soon she turned into the dead end canal where we had seen the exchange between the crabber and Bob. She shot straight past the two side canals and slowed just before the water ended, running the bow up on the bank.

From what I remembered of the satellite overview, this was close to the midpoint of the short side of the canal system. We would have a much better chance of seeing them from there, as well as reaching them if we could. I handed Justine the rifle. I had already seen her handle it safely, but wasn't sure how good a shot she was. Though the long gun would give me an advantage shooting from a distance, the pistol might be ineffective in her hands. Looking up before I stepped off the bow onto the berm, I watched the helicopter approach. It came in from the west and started to circle the system. The fastest way to find Amos would be to follow its lead.

Justine was right behind me with the rifle in the ready position as we climbed the bank to the gravel road. It was hard to know where we were in the canals without any landmarks—except a few weather-beaten trees. My gut told me to head east to find the spot and the helicopter confirmed it a few minutes later.

Two canals ahead, I saw the UTVs parked by the side of the road. Pulling my gun from the holster, I ran toward them signaling to Justine at the same time to stay behind me. She raised the rifle and taking a defensive stance scanned the area. I shouldn't have doubted her abilities. The helicopter was directly overhead and I felt the phone vibrate in my pocket. Ignoring it, I looked up to see who was inside the chopper, but it was too far away. We moved forward.

Three figures came into view as we approached. They were down by the edge of the water on a section of the berm that had eroded, and formed a small flat area. I would have called it a beach except they were ankle-deep in mud. Bob was closest to the edge tossing something into the still water. He had a gallon jug in one hand that I guessed was menhaden oil and a gun in the other. Rebecca stood behind a restrained Amos with the golf club she had hit him with earlier.

Something broke the water about twenty yards from Bob. I could clearly see the armored snout of the crocodile as it approached. Justine pressed close to me and whispered, asking me if she should take it out. I was about to respond in the affirmative when we felt the chopper overhead. The crocodile must have sensed danger and disappeared below the surface before she could take the shot.

The air seemed to come alive around us as the chopper began its descent. It was about fifty feet above us. Bob looked up, and I could see he was trying to decide what to do. Rebecca had no such problem and before I could swing the gun toward her, she wound up and slammed Amos in the head with the golf club. As he fell to the ground, she pushed him forward and into the water. Bob stood frozen, still caught in his indecision. I saw the confusion on his face and knew he was calculating his options. There was zero chance he could escape. When he dropped the gun and raised his hands, I knew he had decided to throw Rebecca under the bus and try and plead out to a lesser charge. Slowly he backed away.

Justine pushed past me as she made a move to the water. I turned, trying to grab her, but it was too late. Amos's body lay face down on the surface. She dropped the rifle on the bank and dove in. Just as she did, I saw a small wake and then two eyes broke the surface of the water. Nothing else mattered to me then, and I moved to the edge of the water and took aim at the crocodile. My finger tightened on the trigger and was just starting to squeeze when the crocodile swam underwater and I lost sight of it. Justine had reached Amos's unconscious body but was only a few feet away from where the croc had disappeared. Without knowing exactly where the croc was it was too dangerous to shoot.

The air seemed to change again and I guessed the chopper had landed. I risked a glance behind me and saw three figures jump from the cockpit. One went toward Bob and the others toward us. Turning back to the water, I searched for the crocodile. There was still no sign of it and I hoped all the activity had scared it away. Justine had Amos on his back with her arm looped around his chest, and was slowly bringing him toward shore. I ran to help.

But before I could say anything, another movement distracted me. With everyone focused on the scene in the water, Rebecca had slid over to where Bob had dropped his gun. I was watching her bend over to pick it up when I felt a movement behind me.

I knew who it was without looking. Her perfume gave her away and I swung my arm one-hundred-eighty degrees hitting the barrel of the rifle. A shot fired, going harmlessly into the air. I stood facing Susan McLeash. My rifle, the one that Justine had dropped before going into the water, was in her hands.

"Kurt, the water," she yelled, raising the barrel again.

I turned and saw the head of the crocodile only inches from Justine. Before Susan could do anything, I took aim with my pistol and fired. I wasn't sure if I had hit the croc when the rifle discharged behind me. Amos's body jerked at the same time as a pool of blood formed where the crocodile had been. It had happened so quickly, I wasn't sure whose shot had gone where.

Justine had kept swimming through the gunshots and reached the bank. Ignoring everything else, I rushed to help her. Knee-deep in the water, I took Amos in a bear hug and had just dragged him onto the bank when another shot was fired.

"You okay?" I asked Justine, then turned to see where the shot had come from.

"Yeah, but he's going to need some help."

Knowing that she was okay, I climbed the bank on all fours. Susan still had the rifle extended in front of her and I saw what she was focused on when I reached the level of the road.

Rebecca was down. Bob's pistol was inches from her hand and Susan was walking toward it. This was all standard procedure except for Susan having my rifle. "Put it down, Susan," I said, moving toward Rebecca. I crawled toward her and picked up the gun. The Miami-Dade officers stood there dumbfounded.

"You're welcome, Hunter," was all Susan said as she lowered the barrel to the ground.

26

There was a long pause while everyone looked around. A lot had happened in a few short seconds. Finally, Justine broke the silence when she called for help.

Amos was conscious now, and she needed extra hands to bring him up to the road where he could be made more comfortable until help arrived. I waited until the two officers were down the bank before I approached Susan.

"The rifle ..." I ordered. Without making eye contact, she handed it to me. Bob was all but forgotten, still standing off to the side where he had remained after he had decided this was his best response. Now, with Rebecca down and the Miami-Dade officers out of sight helping Justine, he got brave and went for one of the UTVs. Without hesitating, I took two shots. Both rear tires took a hit and were flat in seconds. He held his hands up and walked back to the side. "No more nonsense," I said, swinging the barrel of the rifle in his direction for emphasis.

Rebecca's gun lay dangerously close to where he stood. Under normal circumstances I would have asked Susan to retrieve it, but there was no way I was letting her have a gun in her hands. With all I had seen from her in the last few days, I would probably be her next target.

I moved toward the downed body. After placing the pistol in my waistband, I leaned down and saw that Rebecca was dazed, but still alive. The bullet had pierced her shoulder and when I moved her I noticed the clean exit wound. As she sat up, Justine and the two Miami-Dade officers appeared with Amos between them.

"You guys have first aid?" I called to them. "She took a bullet to the shoulder." They placed Amos next to her and while one worked with Justine to make them comfortable, the other went to the helicopter to retrieve a first aid kit.

A few minutes later, two cruisers appeared on the berm near us with an ambulance trailing behind. They pulled up to the scene and I gave Grace a quick rundown. Amos and Rebecca were loaded into the ambulance. Bob was taken into custody and the helicopter took off with Susan in tow. I was glad to be rid of her for now, though I knew I wouldn't get much sleep tonight trying to figure out what to do about her.

Since Justine had been involved, another forensic tech had been called in and we waited, giving our statements to Grace until he arrived. Once the scene was secured and processed, Grace walked over to me, and said goodbye.

Justine and I stood alone on the berm. "You okay?"

"Helluva date."

She leaned against me and I put an arm around her.

27

For better or worse, I had decided to let Susan go. There would be reports written and with the eyewitness corroboration of Justine and the Miami-Dade officers, the truth of what had happened would be beyond dispute. I allowed her some dignity and let her go home.

Now it was Monday morning and I sat across from Martinez. His monitors were off and his attention was fully focused on me. I noticed he wore his dress uniform. Obviously he was expecting some TV time later today.

"That was well done, Hunter," he said. "Miami-Dade's going to get most of the credit, but the park service represented itself well."

The accolades were worthless to me. "Amos and Rebecca are going to be okay," I said, caring more about the people than the publicity. Both had been released from the hospital. Amos was met by his grieving family at the back door, while Rebecca was escorted by Grace Herrera into a Miami-Dade cruiser in front of all three networks' TV cameras. I rarely watched the news, but that was one episode I didn't want to miss. There was still the question of Susan.

"I'll write up my report this morning. Susan has a rather large part in this that I can't ignore."

Martinez looked over at his blank screens. "Ms. McLeash has been reassigned."

I saw the hurt look on his face and didn't press. If she was out of my hair, I was happy. She would appear in the report. At least no one had been killed as a result of her actions, and though she was a bumbling idiot, I didn't think she had done anything that deserved prosecution.

It wasn't often that I had the upper hand with Martinez so as I got up to leave I said, "I've got a bunch of overtime for this. Mind if I take a few days off to balance the books?"

He looked back at me and nodded. My no-budget impact offer was accepted. On the way out I passed the closed door of Susan's office and wondered what reassigned meant. I had other things on my mind though and quickly forgot about her as I went downstairs, waved at Mariposa and headed to the boat.

Justine was there waiting for me. I hopped aboard and released the lines while she started the engine and backed out of the slip. Just as we turned, I saw a group of tourists dressed in bathing suits and bulky PFDs assemble on the dock. The park service ran several snorkeling, kayaking, and sightseeing trips per day and it wasn't an unusual sight until I saw Susan. Dressed in her uniform with a life vest strapped around her chest, she started to talk to the group.

"A little justice," I said to Justine as she pushed down on the throttle. A few minutes later, it was all forgotten when we passed the last marker and the boat went up on plane. I looked over at her and was glad to see that her smile matched mine.

BACKWATER COVE

Get the next book in the Kurt Hunter Mystery Series now:
 Would you commit murder to sign a top high school recruit?...

When National Parks Service special agent Kurt Hunter finds a woman washed up on his remote island in Biscayne National Park the case leads him to the world of high rolling boosters and the young players who will do anything to make their mark.

With millions on the line in the world of college football, recruiting the top names is crucial. Money and women are often used to lure the top high school prospects to schools. With big penalties for getting caught, boosters will do anything—even kill—to cover their tracks and keep their alma maters on top.

Get it now!

Thanks For Reading

If you liked the book please leave a review:

https://www.amazon.com/dp/B078GPQXTM

For more information please check out my web page:
https://stevenbeckerauthor.com/

Or follow me on Facebook:
https://www.facebook.com/stevenbecker.books/

I'm also on Instagram as: stevenbeckerauthor

Get my starter library First Bite for Free!
when you sign up for my newsletter

http://eepurl.com/-obDj

First Bite contains the first book in each of Steven Becker's series:

- Wood's Reef
- Pirate
- Bonefish Blues

By joining you will receive one or two emails a month about what I'm doing and special offers.

Your contact information and privacy are important to me. I will not spam or share your email with anyone.

Wood's Reef

"*A riveting tale of intrigue and terrorism, Key West characters in their* full glory! Fast paced and continually changing direction Mr Becker has me hooked on his skillful and adventurous tales from the Conch Republic!"

Pirate
"A gripping tale of pirate adventure off the coast of 19th Century Florida!"

Bonefish Blues"I just couldn't put this book down. A great plot filled with action. Steven Becker brings each character to life, allowing the reader to become immersed in the plot."

Get them now (http://eepurl.com/-obDj)

Also By Steven Becker

Mac Travis Adventures

Wood's Relic

Wood's Reef

Wood's Wall

Wood's Wreck

Wood's Harbor

Wood's Reach

Wood's Revenge

Wood's Betrayal

Tides of Fortune

Pirate

The Wreck of the Ten Sail

Haitian Gold

Will Service Adventure Thrillers

Bonefish Blues

Tuna Tango

Dorado Duet

Storm Series

Storm Rising

Storm Force

Backwater Series

Backwater Bay

Made in United States
Orlando, FL
01 March 2022